T0198947

OTHER BOOKS WRITTEN:

- ➤ *Playa-i$m*
- ➤ *Psychological Skullduggery*
- ➤ *Political veil: Positioning for power*
- ➤ *That Bitch Called Life*

From the Streets to the Millionaire $eats

"A compelling and motivating story about how a determined nigga plotted, planned, and schemed from the depths of poverty to arrive at the top with riches."

P.Lōs

authorHOUSE®

AuthorHouse™
1663 Liberty Drive
Bloomington, IN 47403
www.authorhouse.com
Phone: 1 (800) 839-8640

This is a work of fiction. All of the characters, names, incidents,
organizations, and dialogue in this novel are either the products
of the author's imagination or are used fictitiously.

Published by AuthorHouse 12/21/2018

ISBN: 978-1-5462-6314-2 (sc)
ISBN: 978-1-5462-6313-5 (e)

Print information available on the last page.

Contents

"I have never asked you this before, how were you able to achieve some much with an unprivileged rocky start? You weren't born rich, but now you are!"

This story will pull your emotions, twist your mind, and leave you spellbound. You will wonder or think, how can a person be ruthless, heartless, cunning and achieve their goals, in a world of cut-throats, liars, cheaters and successful manipulators. If you can understand deeply within your soul on what it takes to be rich and successful, then you also have what it takes to be the next millionaire!!!

The Sponge

Carlo "The Wiz" Rodgers woke up at his usual time at 5 am. He went into the kitchen, and turned on the coffee maker to prepare him a cup of coffee. Next, he went into the bathroom and took a shit and then jumped in the shower. His beautiful wife, that has been by his side for ten years plus, was still lying in bed. After drying off, and making his way to the large elaborate closet. He jumped into some hard creased khakis that loosely fitted his medium waist. Then, he slipped on a crisp and clean white T-shirt that he always tucked in. Then he slid his feet into some soft white socks, that complimented his casual Italian slippers, that were so soft it was as though he was walking on balls of cotton.

Carlo "The Wiz" was a dark coconut skin brother, with a bald head, and medium height, but was a giant among his peers with great admiration for money and success. He headed back to the kitchen, when he entered the huge kitchen, his beautiful wife Sunshine Rogers was wrapped in her silk pink robe with a gleaming smile on her youthful caramel face. She was so appealing, she didn't wear make-up. Plus, her husband didn't like for her to wear make-up. He always believed that heavy make-up hides or covers God's masterful hand work, when it came to Black women. Mrs. Sunshine Rogers was a retired teacher. She taught sixth grade Reading and Social Studies. She knew from growing up in those black ostracized days of Black America, that the public school was a joke. When she attended college, she saw the depths of the game within the system when it came to education. Plus, the school text books were old and beaten. She admired education, and loved reading herself, which was a great passion of hers. She understood greatly, that the best education, was self-education. When one truly educates him or herself willfully learns more, because of the desire to know. She didn't like the public school educational system, but she endured it for 13 years. She knew what she taught her students was a downtrodden political set-up of the American system called education that was bias, unbalanced, uncivil, ethical prejudices and a designed failed system for Blacks and Hispanics to be step-up for failure. When it came to men, her father taught her that all men wanted one thing from a woman. Mrs. Rodgers and her two sisters couldn't go any where, unless it was to church, to school or other family homes. Her father's words did come true when she first started teaching. That was when the principal of the Middle School where she taught, he tried to make a move on her. The thing that made her father's words reign supremely true, was the way the principal threw himself at her. All of his comments and gestures were sexually provocative. Mrs. Rodgers had to threaten him about sexual harassment in order for him to back-up and even stop. Also, when she attended college her best friend was raped by an all-star football player her sophomore year. Her best friend never finished her college studies to also become a teacher. Until this very day Mrs. Rodger's best friend continues to take psychotropic medications due to her depression, and paranoia state of mind. She continues to see a psychologist on a monthly bases. These two hurtful experiences made an impact on Mrs. Sunshine Rodger's early life to be very cautious and careful went it came to men. She had become so careful and cautious like most people that are too cautious that it becomes fear, and no progress can be made through fear. She was afraid to make a step in the arena of cordial relationships, but eventually that would all changed, due to one suave and smooth guy, that understood the physiological make-up of women. When she met her husband twenty some odd years ago, her father's concepts of men changed. Carlo "The Wiz" Rodgers understood that women have an insatiable emotional need, and wanting that has a strong desire to be fulfilled. He also understood that relationships between couples was no different than warfare or business. One always tried to get the upper hand or the best position to get the other person to be what they wanted or needed before the battle can cease. Which means in the beginning of most relationships, there's a lot of cautious pretensions, manipulation and charm being orchestrated and cloaked with an appeal of respect wrapped in cleverness. Since, he understood the desires of women, it was that much easier for him to capture Sunshine Mosley. So, Carlo "The Wiz" used her feminine desire against her to fuel more desire for him. He would turn down her sex whenever they went out on dates. He would stay away or be absent for long periods of time. He made sure that he would call her in between these times, to keep his bait on the hook. When the appropriate time came, all he had to do was reel her in. Whenever they got together, he would make sure she had the greatest time of her life. She would always find herself yearning for his company. He played the yo-yo and push-pull game with her. The more he played this game the more she tried to keep him in her sight and proximity. The way he played the game made her father's words appear irrelevant to him, and she was swept off her feet as we say. Mrs. Rodgers has been by her husband's side from that moment on.

She was cooking them breakfast, which consisted of French toast, eggs and bacon. She was the apple of his eyes. She was caramel tone beautiful with a bold graceful feminine appeal. Her voice was like an innocent little girl when she spoke, but she was very intelligent. Her intelligence is what captured Carlo "The Wiz" the most. Beauty and intelligence was his greatest attraction when it came to women, but when it came to socializing with men of a certain caliber he took it very seriously. Carlo "The Wiz" didn't like to socialize with men that were raw, ruthless without brains and cunning. He believed that a razor edge mentality with high intelligence - with a goal, gave men purpose and value. Without intelligence or a goal, you were just as useless as a broke down vehicle with four flat tires. To Carlo "The Wiz," a man without goals and wits was a useless being. Any person that is useless always winds up in the way for those that see progression, from the streets to the corporate seats. These types of reckless people always made it difficult or cause the Rollers to crack down on real hustlers and players with a plan. Growing up he saw how the ruthless, the rawness and abrasive actions destroyed a man and his family, whether by death or life imprisonment. Seeing Black men losing their lives and their little freedom over petty crimes, was a great lesson to Carlo "The Wiz" when he was coming up. He always told himself, that some women are sexy without beauty, but very few women are beautiful, sexy, classy and intelligent, which he considered were the highest traits of a real lady. Mrs. Rogers went to the bathroom, and took her shower. Then, she slipped on a beautiful yellow and white flower summer dress that hung down to her ankles. She put on some sweet lotion that smelled like cotton candy, that made her flawless body just glow with erotic ecstasy. Next, she slid her well pedicure feet into some casual sandals. Her and husband were both taught from their families and the old school elders about style and grace, mannerism, dressing presentable, speaking intelligently, respecting yourself, having the upper most respect for the elderly, and revering your people no matter, if they were educated or uneducated, poor or rich they were your people. Carlo "The Wiz" was in the kitchen fixing his coffee, when his wife entered the kitchen smelling like sweet cotton candy, and looking like a caramel toasted almond. She always aroused her husband's sexual desire, because of her beauty, grace and mannerism as a lady. She knew her husband loved her dearly, and one thing she knew most of all concerning her husband, was that he never was insecure. They both sat down, and ate their breakfast. She admired her husband greatly. Her husband was a very confident man, and a very deep thinker. That was one of the main things she loved about him the most. No one could change his mind, even if they challenged his ideas or plans. When it came to Carlo's great plans and strategies for his future, he never made decisions out of anger, or without considering the cost or consequences of those decisions. He respected everyone's frankness of truth. But he never revealed his true intentions or thoughts.

She walked over, and gave him a sweet passionate kiss. At that moment his rod began to rise, and she became moist in between those luscious beautiful shapely caramel thighs. After finishing their breakfast, and preparing another cup of coffee, and they both walked onto the front porch of their big beautiful huge home, that consisted of five bedrooms, four and a half bath, a study, an office, a den and also a party or media room. Their home sat on the out skirts on Loot Street, that ran down to Bottom Blvd. of the black neighborhood. Carlo "The Wiz" chose to live there, because he always had love for his people, and wanted to be near them. Even though his people didn't show much love for each other or for him at times, but those were his people. Carlo "The Wiz" knew that Black on Black death was due to slavery, and the slave masters' teachings. Slavery was a tool of psychological destructiveness taught by so-called "Willie Lynch" and other slave masters to implement hatred of self and your people. But when it came to loving and respecting your masters' wishes at all cost, has trickled down to this present day. We can see and witness the killings, drugging, robbing and destruction of Black lives. It's a geopolitical-economic set-up of deprivation, when it comes to Black lives. Many of us know this, and yet we don't push or implement the same horrific treatment that made them millions and billions of dollars, or what they considered Old Money. Blacks have been taught to look down on players, hustlers and pimps. When it comes to this United States economical system, it operates from the components of the oldest profession, known as prostitution and pimping. The whores are the workers or the employees, the customer are considered the foolish tricks, the john or customer, and the CEO or Business Owner is the pimp or top-player. We know who owns the systems, the banks, the politics of powerful influence, and we all know the system is created by the rich, for the rich and they don't play fair, but that's the game. Those that play long enough with determination usually wins parts and shares of those riches. The ones that hate or blame, are the lames that lose in this game of life and success.

Carlo "The Wiz" was a young sponge when he was coming up in the hood. Whenever elders, streets cats and economical-political figures spoke from podiums on television, or streets corners he made it his priority to listen. He didn't understand why Blacks could kill their own potential tribal leaders, their possible warrior brothers or their capable business partners. He considered the hustlers, players, con men, pimps and smart street niggas were his closes ally and family, that did what they had to in order to make a living for themselves. Getting his hands dirty with crack, heroin or other destructible drugs is something he always despised, because of all the collateral damage that came with it, in the Black communities. To him Blacks wasn't using their God-given intelligence correctly. Then, they wondered why their kids' kids were caught up in that vicious cycle called self-destruction or self-sabotage. Carlo "The Wiz" never did wanted kids, he reasoned why would any person bring a child or children into this nasty selfish cruel cold upside down world.

That was too late for him. His daughter Melody Lorenzo that he loved very much, looked like her mother's twin. She had that serious shrewd mental keenness of her father. She was a University student when she met and married Ralph Lorenzo. They dated for two years before they got married. Melody is going to school to be a doctor, and her husband was working at warehouse distribution, and attending night school, at the local community college for engineering. Melody and her husband always joked about the first time Ralph Lorenzo met her parents. She warned Ralph about her father's seriousness when it came to goals and being a man. When Ralph met his wife's father Carlo "The Wiz", for the first time his knees were shaking like jelly, and his throat was rough and dry, which made it impossible for him to speak clearly. Ralph was very nervous when he met his father-in-law. Thanks to Melody's mother Mrs. Rodgers, she helped Ralph make it through that old time father's interrogation, that all young men have to endure when it comes to daddy's littler girl or girls. Melody and her husband lived in one of her father's properties that he owned. She didn't have to pay rent or the yearly taxes. It was a one-story brick home with four bedrooms, three in half baths, a medium size kitchen, ten feet high ceiling in the living room, a study and wooden floors throughout the house. Their home was across the tracks, on Green Clover Rd. in a mix suburban district. Melody and Ralph had one child that was five-years old, Carlo Lorenzo was her son's name. She named their son after her father. Carlo "The Wiz" and his grand-child spent quality time together whenever he wasn't in school, with his parents or playing with his friends. When Melody graduated from high school her father bought her a brand new luxury coupe, and he also opened a bank account for her with the amount $50,000, and there was more money if she needed it. His wife and him made sure that their daughter didn't have to be a victim or predator of their own people's calamities, which causes us to prey upon each other, or be victimize one way or another. Carlo "The Wiz" never sold drugs to his people, that was something he vowed to never do no matter how hard it was. He didn't knock other street hustlers, if selling drugs was the hustler's hustle, so be it. To him that was genocide, and playing the game for the man that wanted all Blacks to be dope fiends and hopeless junkies with no aspirations for a great and meaningful life.

He took a sigh when he sat down in his rocking chair that was on the front porch. Neighborhood people would sometimes stop, and converse with his wife and him about things going on in the streets and around the community. This morning was a very nice day. A nice cool breeze was blowing, the air smelled fresh and clean, the sun was shinning warmly, and the birds were singing their morning songs on the beauty of creation. While the hood people were groping, some were begging, others were moping, planning, complaining, drinking, drugging, hustling and all the other vices came with the street life, called survival. The politicians were doing their thing on Capital Hill and in the White House from Congress down to the state senators, city mayors, city officials, connected lawyers and the police department called politicking for power, control and money. To Carlo "The Wiz," that was all part of the game call life. He knew from experience that corporate businesses wasn't no different than the streets of cunning, manipulation and cut-throat gamming for the sharp determine person to win.

After taking a few sips of hot coffee, Carlo went back into the house to roll him up some of that superb herb. When he sat down again, he looked over at his wife. She had her legs crossed looking so gracefully appealing with a certain look on her face like something was weighing heavy on her mind. Carlo "The Wiz" asked, "Baby, what's wrong? You got this look on your face as though something is occupying your deepest thoughts." She grinned a little and replied, "It's nothing." Carlo knew when his wife, or anyone for that matter was trying to pull bullshit over on him, or just held back their questions. That was something that ran him raggedy in an instant. He didn't like for people to make mention of something or start to say something, and then state it's nothing or forget about it. Carlo "The Wiz" looked over his right shoulder at her again, and he was a little heated under his collar as we say. Carlo "The Wiz" never allowed himself to loose his cool, or let anyone make him too angry to lose focus on the angle or the next move that is always imperative to tacticians. Beauty and riches don't compare to information or knowledge, which are the two most precious things to value other than life its self. She said,

"Honey do you think our people will ever get themselves together. I mean, when you study our history it's amazing how our people were prosperous with horrendous acts of racial bigotry, hatred, lynching, murdering, assassinations and denying Blacks economical and political autonomy to prosper as a people is appalling? Our people back in the days did good even with all the odds stacked up against them, and they still overcame those odds. Now today, with all this so-called freedom our people don't have their minds right, and we are against each other economically, politically and spiritually. Something is very wrong in our people's psychology and unified moral sentiments." Carlo "The Wiz" just looked at his wife for a moment before he answered. Then he stated, "Well, as the saying goes times makes the man, and the man makes his life according to what he eats and digest." His wife replied, "Honey what do food have to do with how a people or person thinks and acts?" He just laughed at her comment, then spoke, "No baby. What I mean is, whatever a man thinks and believes is the thing he acts on. What he eats is his words that he speaks, and those words becomes his psychology to act on that fuel of his words, thoughts and feelings. You dig?" She replied, "Oh, okay honey I see. You didn't have to get all philosophical on me. I know you are an intelligent man."

Minutes later their daughter Melody drove up in the driveway with her black luxury coupe shinning and sparkling clean. She walked up onto the steps and kissed and hugged her father, and then her mother. Her father asked, "Where's my boy?" His daughter replied, "He's at home with his father. They are getting ready to go play flag football with some of his co-workers and their boys some where. So, I thought I would come over and see what my love-bugs were up to." Her father stated, "Nothing baby-girl just out here enjoying this beautiful day. How is school going?" Melody answered, "It's going good. I had to go to the book store, and buy a book I needed for one of my classes." Then her mother told her, "If you need a book or books and they are too expensive, you tell us so we can get them for you. I know those books can very expensive. Okay, baby?" Melody was sitting on the arm of her mother's chair looking like a honey dipped almond with shinning charcoal colored hair that hung down her back. She responded to her mother last statement, "I know mom, I know. I will ask if I need to." Melody looked at her father as he was pulling on that good smoke. She asked her father, "Daddy, I never asked you this before. "How were you able to achieve some much without going to college and with a unprivileged rocky start? You weren't born rich but now you are! That has been on my mind for quite a while now. I just decided to ask." Carlo "The Wiz" just laughed. He was in a mellow mood. He knew his daughter wasn't a street person by all means. She came from a very good sheltered life, due to her parents' strict and fair code of conduct. He replied, "Well baby, that's a long story." Mrs. Rogers stated, "No one has to go to a job, so we got all the time in the world, honey." All three of them just laughed. Freedom from having money struggles is always an elating feeling of achievement. Especially for Blacks that have to continue to fight for their amendments rights, in a so-called free society. Being Black in America with millions of dollars and influence makes it that much rewarding to the Black soul called Black Heaven.

Carlo "The Wiz" took a pull off his gangster green again, and looked over at his wife and daughter. He thought to himself that all the lessons and game he learned as a youngster with goals and dreams paid off. He no longer have to look over his shoulders, and feel some form of paranoia if he made a right or wrong decision. He always thought things through from all angles when it came to making strategic survival plans. He said to himself with a little grin on his face, *'what and how am I going to reveal this story to my child.'* His wife noticed he had this little devilish smile on his face. She always called it the devil's grin. He tried to respond, but he couldn't, due to that superb herb. His mental recollection of pulling off all types of schemes without getting caught up, brought a joy to his inner being. As he sat looking around, and pondered what a beautiful life it is to be a Black multi-millionaire just tickled him greatly.

Sweet BBQ

Melody asked, "Dad are you going to tell me how you became rich." Her father replied, "Well I guess I will have to since you asked. Can you run down to Kelly's Meat Market and pick up some chicken legs and wings, and turkey sausage so I can put some on the BBQ pit. When you get back, we can all sit out back and have a family day. Then, I will tell you what you want to know sweetie." Melody jumped in her car, and backed out the driveway. Mr. and Mrs. Rodgers went into the house to get things ready for the pit. They both were in the kitchen, when Carlo 'The Wiz" asked his wife, "Do you think I should tell her how I became rich?" His wife replied, "Well, you told her you would tell her, and plus she has the right to know what her father did to become rich." Carlo "The Wiz", went to the garage to grab the bag of charcoal and starter fluid. Then, he headed to the backyard where he had a large gazebo built, and next to the gazebo was built a bar with a sink, bottle rack for imported wines and liquor, that was fully stocked. The BBQ pit was about fifteen feet away from the luxury gazebo, due to the large backyard. It had several amazing comfortable relaxing lounging chairs, and outside short table to place drinks on. Also, inside the built up gazebo, he had an expensive stereo system built inside that was very accessible to remove whenever the weather got nasty. While Carlo "The Wiz," was pouring the coals in the pit, and pouring the starter fluid on the coals. His mind was searching and seeking the means, and ways to tell his daughter the story of his past. He knew his daughter loved him greatly, but he also knew how people didn't understand certain things would condemn them, or see the means as negative.

Carlo "The Wiz's" daughter was a bright and sharp woman for her age. When he first told his wife the story of his life before they got married, she understood greatly because of her own struggles and triumphs. That's why very few black people are rich, they focus on the how and not the why. Then, they wonder why they arrive at their desired end, which is caught up in the how, which is like a ball of twisted yarn. Carlo "The Wiz" stood over the pit when he threw the match on the fluid soaked coals, as the fire blazed for a moment before it simmered. His mind was still flipping and flapping concerning on how he was going to tell his daughter about his corporate exploits. He understood that the American system was built on exploiting its citizens for the cookies, and the citizens received the crumbs from their political-corporate masters' tables. He also understood the game was rigged and set-up for the rich and by the rich. Mrs. Rodgers called him several times before he responded to her call. "Yes," he replied back to her, while she was standing in between the backdoor and the kitchen. She yelled, "Do you need anything from the kitchen?" He just shook his head no. He walked back over to the gazebo, and sat down letting the pit fire and smoke level out.

Carlo "The Wiz" laid back in one of the lounging chairs relaxing, and thinking to himself, that he was about to relive his past. It can be alright reminiscing with close friends, shooting the shit with down partners, other than telling a love one the reality without the ego shuck and jive that hood cats do with pride concerning their hustles. Especially, when they were the winners of those survival cunning methods, mixed with male boasting was fulfilling emotionally with psychological gratification to a certain degree. Minutes later, his wife was bring out the back door with her a pan full of seasoned meats, which indicated his daughter was back. Melody his daughter came out behind her mother with a glass, a bottle of bourbon and water, and also with his superb-herb can. He stated, "How did you know I wanted that?" They both laughed a little then she replied, "Mom told me you probably was going to want it. So, you wouldn't have to go back and forward. Plus, I thought I would save you a trip." Carlo "The Wiz" looked at his daughter's expression and demeanor to get a feel on how she was feeling, which meant he was sizing up his daughter emotional state of being at the time. It's all instinctual street tactics to size up people or try to get a feel on where they were psychologically and emotionally. He slid out of the lounging chair. He told his wife and daughter, "I'll be back I have to use the restroom." She thought to herself what is wrong with my dad, he's telling me he has to used the restroom. She replied, "Okay. I'll be here." He kissed her on the cheek, and walked into the house. He knew this was it, the moment has arrive to relive his past. He washed his hands, and then took a piss. That was an old habit he picked up, which fed his mind. That it's all about keeping a clean dick, and looked into the mirror. He poked out his chest, and said in a loud mumbling tone, *'I am intelligent, and my daughter will understand. If she doesn't well it's too damn late Wiz. You did your dirt, and washed your hands with it. So live and let live.'* The Wiz was the street name he got during his heydays, and until this very day streets cats and friends still calls him "The Wiz." They all knew he was a player, a big womanizer, but never a pimp.

Then, he headed back to the back yard where his wife and daughter were sitting out back. Before going out back, he swooped into the garage, and retrieved the large outdoor fan, and rolled it to the back facing the gazebo. He went back to the garage to grabbed the long electrical cord, and plugged the large fan up, and then turned the switch on. When he turned the fan knob control on medium, his wife and daughter both just sighed with, 'Ah that feels better.' Even though it was a beautiful day, and the sun began to really rise with intensity. Then, he walked over to the large pit where the meat were sitting on the BBQ pit stand. The BBQ was smoking good and evenly heated. He placed all the meat on the hot grill, and went over where his wife and daughter were sitting to take a seat.

Carlo "The Wiz" poured himself a drink of bourbon and water, and rolled him up a nice gangster green smoke. When he it lit up the superb-herb his daughter stated, "Okay dad, I am ready to hear how you became the man you are now concerning the money and lifestyle." Carlo "The Wiz" blew smoke out of his nose and looked at his daughter and wife with this grin on his face. Okay, baby I'll say this, "Sometimes bad situations and the wrong choices can be the very thing that turns out good, and become the right answer for a purpose, you dig what I'm saying?" His daughter replied, "I understand. I'm love you no matter what." After about forty-five minutes, he got up to take a few pieces of the chicken legs off the pit for his wife and daughter to taste. Then her father asked his daughter and wife how is the BBQ. Melody replied, "It's good. You know we always liked your BBQ sweet man, ha, ha." Then his wife commented, "You use a different sauce or something this time. It made the meat taste kind of sweet, and plus with a little tinge of spice. It was a good balance of sweet and spice. But it was more sweet than spicy. Baby you know I love it whenever you BBQ. We need to do this a little more often. With the craziness going in the world today, we need to make more time for each other." Carlo "The Wiz" got out of his lounging chair, and went over and hugged his wife and daughter. He told them, "I want the both of you to listen carefully. I love both you from depths of my soul, and everything that I will do, and have done is for my family to live very comfortable, and also make sure that my grand-son can have a good life. Baby-girl I'm not trying to tell you how to raise your son, if you are going to spoil him, you make sure that you make him work for it or earns everything he wants. Giving kids or anybody something easily, makes them lazy and ungrateful, you dig?" She replied, "Dad I know, mother and you wasn't easy on me, so I know." Then, Carlo "The Wiz" kissed the both of them again.

On Deck

"Well, baby-girl when I was in the 12th grade, my father was very ill, and my mother had past three years before that. My father worked at this Mining Company for seventeen years. So, he had to stop working due to his illness. The bad thing is that the company didn't want to give him his full retirement benefits, because he didn't give the company twenty years to get the full benefits. The insurance only paid a certain amount, and the money was getting low. I took a job at the local grocery-store. Uncle Willie helped as much as he could, because he retired from the postal service, but he was also battling with cancer. I was forced to take a job, and take care of my father. I would work nights, and go to school from there. I must admit, I would fall asleep in class, but this little female had a crush on me. I used her to my advantage to get her to do my homework. She would always sit in front of me in two of our classes. That way she would pass me the answers, or let me look on her paper. She would lean to one side when the teachers wasn't looking in order for me to copy her paper. Uncle Willie had two kids, and his daughter was on drugs real bad, and he was paying some of her bills and paid for her to go to several rehabs. Janet

"Super-Head" Smith. She took her mother's last name, but her brother Willie Nathaniel Rodgers Jr got his name from their father. "Super-Head" had two kids while she was living on Section 8." Melody interrupted, "Excuse me dad, why did they call her Super-Head?" Carlo "The Wiz" laughed, "Well baby-girl let me say it like this. When it came to performing a sexual act, they said she could suck like a vacuum, you dig?" Melody bellowed, "Oh how nasty and gruesome! Man, I never understood how some women could do that type of stuff!" Carlo "The Wiz" said, "Well baby-girl, it all depends on the reasons and point why a woman will do it. We'll talk about that much later or some other time. Or maybe you and your mother can have that conversation among yourselves." His wife just laughed and then replied, "You the expert on that typed of matter." He played it down, "Yet right! Anyway, she was found dead due to a drug overdose in her apartment. Which was a one bedroom apartment with no food in the refrigerator and no bed. When Uncle Willie and the cops entered the apartment the stench was so foul and wretched it smelt like a dead animal." Melody asked her father, "How long was she dead before they found her?" Her father replied, "I think uncle Willie said she had been there four or five days according to the autopsy investigation." Melody's left cheek was moist, due to a tear rolling down her beautiful almond coconut cheek. Her mother rubbed her back to console her. Carlo "The Wiz" continued, "Anyway the only furniture she had was a table in the kitchen with one chair, a love sofa, and the lights were off. The kids were in CPS custody, due to her drug habit. Uncle Willie and Pops tried to adopt the kids, but due to their age and illness, the State wouldn't let that happen. If mother or Aunt Rita hadn't passed earlier, the situation for the kids would have been much better and different. After the family tragedy, then cousin Willie Jr, passed from a cirrhosis of the liver due to his heavy drinking. Junior, was seeing a psychologist twice a month, and with all the medications he took, it didn't help. His mental state was slipping rapidly from paranoia. He always thought that somebody was out to kill him. Junior, became a die-hard alcoholic. Trying to help his daughter, and his son Willie Jr, and my father was draining Uncle Willie pockets. Plus, Uncle Willie was older than Pops. Anyway, my father was loosing a lot of weight. So, I would go down to the juke-joints, and cop some superb-herb for my father. That was the only thing that helped my father gain his weight back, and endure the pain. He had what they called the black-lung, from working in that mining business for so many years. So, one night uncle Willie couldn't make it. I called off. I didn't go to work. I told the store-manager that I had to study for a major test. The store manager understood that. So, I stayed home with Pops. We sat up talking, and smoking that superb-herb. While sitting there with the Old Man, I was internally thinking *what am I going to do, if the Old Man dies now.* I had this inner anger within me about how my father gave his life and time to that company for almost twenty years, and he couldn't receive his full retirement benefits. To me that was the worst form of robbery or humiliation. I told myself, that *I would be a multi-millionaire.* Just like they used my father up, I was going to use every breathe in my body from the streets all the way up the ladder to the corporate seats, to never become a victim of poverty."

"I went to the joke-joint the next night, since Uncle Willie was feeling a little better. I didn't care about that job. I went for a few hours, played like I was sick, because I didn't want my father to know that I was hanging out. My father was from that life, and he had encountered numerous life threatening situations for being in that life. Even though many of us know this lifestyle is dangerous mentally and physically. He was shot three times, stabbed five times." Melody interrupted, "Why and what happen, for grand-dad to get shot or stabbed?" Her father continued, "He told me that he beat this one guy so many times shooting pool and playing for money. The bet got bigger, and the guy didn't want to pay up. So, the guy was talking trash, and threaten to kill my father. Then, the Old Man hit him, and the guy fell to the floor, as he was getting up slow. The Old Man kicked him again, and turned to leave. When my Old Man walked off, the guy came running from behind him, and started stabbing him. The joke-joint owner broke it up, about that time he pulled that guy off Pops, when the Old Man had suffered five stab wounds. They had to rush him to the hospital, and the doctor told him, that he lost so much blood, that if the paddy-wagon would have been a minute late, he would have died in route. Mrs. Rodgers asked, "Whatever happened to the guy that stabbed dad?" Carlo "The Wiz", replied to his wife question, "The Old Man told me three years later after that, the guy was found dead in an alley, from a bullet shot in the back of the head. That's an indication of a orchestrated hit or assassination for large sums unpaid of money. A great message was sent to the rest of the borrowers and beggars that didn't pay their points or principal of the money they owed. Everybody knew my Old Man didn't take no shit. He also spoke to me about having respect and class as a street hustler or player, but not everyone can and would stick to the code." Melody put her hand over her mouth, and said, "Oh, my God! No one went to jail for that?" Then, Carlo "The Wiz" continued, "Come on baby-girl, we don't snitch on each other. We handle shit our own way. Anyway, he told me he was shot one night by a jealous cat, called "Snake." Mother and him was just coating at the time, you dig? They weren't married yet, and this cat called "Snake." He said the guy kept hitting on mother, but she wouldn't give him no play. One night they went out dancing, because moms liked to dance. So, that same cat "Snake" was there at the juke-joint when they were out just having some fun dancing and socializing. Her and Pops were sitting at a table having a drink, and that same cat "Snake" came over to the table. Pops said he was amp-ed up. My mother told him to leave her alone, but he wouldn't. Then, my father told him to step off, and show some respect. The guy threw up his hands in a surrendering gesture, as though everything was cool and backed off. He stumbled out of the front door. About an hour later, my Old Man said when they were leaving. Father went to open the door for mother, and when he came back around to get in the car on his side, someone called his name. Which was "Stomp." Mrs. Rodgers interjected, "Why did they call daddy Stomp?" Carlo "The Wiz", responded to his wife's question, "Old Man wasn't no pimp or major player, he just had a way with women, he was rigid without compromising, no-nonsense, wisely arrogant, stood by his principles of what a man should be, peaceful but daring, and quite but commanding. It was all principal with him. When guys tried to knock him, or steal the woman he was with, they couldn't. Which was the way he handled himself, which was tight, hard and there was not cracks in his ways of handling his business or relationships with the women he dated or how he dealt with people. So, they started calling him Stomp-Down. Some of the street cats call him SD, Stomp-Down or just Stomp. When the guy called the Old Man's name he stepped from behind the large trash bin, and just commenced to squeezing that trigger. Mother drove him to the nearest hospital. The Old Man, damn near died again. After that, him and mother got married, and he left the street life of hustling and womanizing for good. When the cops came to the hospital to question the Old Man about the incident, he told the cops that someone tried to rob him. Mother and him told the cops that they didn't really see his face, because it was too dark, and the guy had ran off when mother started screaming and yelling. She had to run around to the driver-side of the car. That's when someone stepped out of the club, and ran back into the club to call the paddy wagon." Carlo's daughter was just puzzled and baffled about what she was hearing. Plus, she knew that when her father told stories, he told them with great details, and plus in a way that was just moving, tantalizing and emotionally driven whenever he told them. Then, she asked her father, "What happened to the guy that shot grand-dad?" He responded, "I think the Old Man, told me he was doing life in the pen for murder with a deadly weapon, and strong arm-robbery at a bank. He supposedly had shot a bank-teller. I think that's what the Old Man told me or uncle Willie. Hold on for a second let me check this pit, and see how this meat is doing. Baby, can you grab a pan so this sausage can come off the pit." Mrs. Rodgers got up went into the kitchen to retrieve a pan for her husband. Carlo "The Wiz", started putting the sausage links into the pan, and took the pan of meat into the house, and made him a quick sandwich. Then he went back to where is daughter and wife were still sitting. Carlo "The Wiz" took a sigh and sat back down. Melody stated, "Dad are you going to finish telling me the story?" He looked at his daughter and wife, replied, "Yes baby-girl. I am trying to make this story short as possible." Mrs. Rodgers replied, "Honey like I said before, no one has a job to go to." Carlo "The Wiz" just shook his head, and continued telling his story.

"So, one night I ran into this cat named "Spoons" down on Windy Street, which was who I would cop my herb from. I asked him who could I rap to about the game of cop, lock and control. "Spoons" and I was sitting in his ride, which was a Black-chromed out spaceship. I said, "Spoons my man. I have been copping that herb from you for a minute now. I got to have some game on who's the top player out here." Spoons" turned and looked at me like I was the biggest damn fool with his maroon eyes glued on me. "Spoons" commented with humor of seriousness, "Lil nigga you got to be jiving! Man ain't one nigga is going to give you game to cut into his playing field of getting scratch. Yeah, it's fucking hotter than hell out here on the streets nigga. These niggas out here are Hell-bound! Shit the Devil don't have shit compared to these niggas. Look here lil nigga, these niggas out here are so cold, the Devil don't come down here because he got them shook and hooked. God through his wisdom see that it would be useless to come down here trying to break these niggas' from the Devil's charm and harm. Niggas see paper, not God. Ain't no nigga going to believe in something he can't touch or use for a money tool, you dig? Because out here, it's hell getting bread, and it's paradise having major bread. The other level of hell is breaking and controlling bitches, getting money in all forms and fashions, shooting and killing hating ass niggas that's trying to block or stop another niggas' hustle, and finding ways to get over on the next nigga, you dig where I'm coming from?" I said, "I dig that. My game is for the bigger fish, and a much more sophisticated hustle." Spoons just laughed, "Nigga, what you mean more sophisticated?" I was about to tell the nigga what I meant, but then the nigga kept rapping. "Man the best sophisticated nigga out here is them god-damn players and old school hustlers. Hell even some of them don't play by the rules no more." Then he asked me a question. "Do you know why there ain't no rules out on these war-infested bloody streets?" I just shook my head yes. He said, "Why?" I replied, "Because no one respects the game or the rules of the game." He looked at me and commented, "Naw nigga! I peeped game out here. Every nigga out here wants to do his shit his way. No nigga wants to be told what he can and can't do, and then money is the shit everybody is trying to get their claws on. Every nigga is preying on another nigga in this wretched filthy cesspool of everyday struggle called the hood, that's why. Whenever money is tight, it makes niggas ruthless, hard and cold, because without that paper you are in a bad shape. Especially, if you are use to having paper, and then shit gets tight. Then, you got those crooked ass Rollers, out here getting free pussy from them whores, and making them D-boys break off some of that bread or get popped. Then them lame ass snitches go to the singing like a mocking-birds." I looked at "Spoons," and stated, "That's why I want to rap with top-players because, I'm use all the game they run-down to me, and take that shit inside the corporate world." Spoons lit up a gangster-green, and took a pull off that good smelling superb-herb. He was seven years my senior, and a young cat with facial features of an old man with a face of a drooped bag of struggle, hardships, pain and agony was written all over his young corpse. He was words were real and painful, with much anger because of the life he had to endure on a day to day bases. Even today, us hood niggas can witness this everyday pain, economic anguish and torn souls of restless hardships. "Spoons" said, "Nigga, I knew you was a damn fool when I first met you. You get to fucking around with them white bitches, and they yell rape on your ass, whether you did it or not. They going to believe her because she is white, and they going to give your stupid ass the electric chair, fuck the death penalty with a needle. They going to bring that chair back for your stupid green ass. Nigga, I going step into this club. You can keep that joint." I got out with Spoons, and leaned against the side of the car pulling on the gangster-green, when he asked was I coming in. I told him that I would a little later. My mind was zipping and zapping from that superb-herb, and I was thinking deeply about my goals and destiny." Melody interrupted, "You knew what part? Part of what?" Carlo The Wiz", said, "If I were to F-up with any white person male or female in that corporate world, my ass would be grass, if I screwed up severely. I was very determine to make it, and I didn't want to play the game my people were playing on each other. I always heard that street knowledge was heavier than Harvard schooling, but how many of us really put it to the test. Very few of our people made it to the top without a college degree. That concealed my fate, to keep it moving."

"The Old Man died about a year later after I graduated from high school, and Uncle Willie died two years after that. I am glad that Pops did get to see me graduate from high school. Pops didn't finish high school. Melody asked, "Why grand-dad didn't finish school?" He stated, "Pops and his father didn't have a good enough relationship, and Pops told me he left at the age of 14, and been on his on every since. That's why he was rigid and streets-wise. He graduated from the University of Concrete Jungle" Carlo "The Wiz", continued, "Uncle Willie willed his house to me, and I remained living in the home I grew up in. Working at the grocery-store wasn't going to keep up the maintenance and taxes on both homes. So, I had to figure out a few things, which lead me to my reality that I really didn't know a damn thing. So, I was going down to the club Pink Pony, which was on Windy Street on a regular bases. I needed that knowledge on how to be suave and smooth with tactics. Possessing those traits of skills of getting money, and knowing what to do with the money once you get it is one of the most important disciplines of having money. The Old Man died with $3,500 dollar in his bank account, and Uncle Willie had $1,800 in his account. I took this money that was willed to me, and went to the Men's Luxury Store to cop me two nice looking cheap suits and shoes, and then a gold pinky ring trying to look hip. Then, I was going to the book-stores, and I started reading books on psychology, investing and leadership. I sold the Old Man's Fleetwood Caddy, and used the money to fix up Uncle Willie's house to rent out. I went to the bank, and opened a business account. I still lived in the family house. I started going to business seminars and back to the Pink Pony club. I quit the grocery-store job. The good thing at the time, is that I had some respected middle age family that was renting Uncle Willie's house. That was a steady source of money coming in at that time. I had to make a quick move, because you didn't know when your tenants would move out. One night while at the Pink Pony, I was peeping game, when Spoons walked in. "What's happening lil nigga? What you doing up in here? Oh, you trying to get your coat pulled on game." Spoons pointed at this blue-black nigga that was decked in a leather black suit, with his lid cocked ace-duce. We leaned into each other trying to hear one another, due to the music that was loud. He said, "That's Black Jack, one of the coldest hustlers out here. The nigga about sixty or damn near seventy years old, but he's still sharp. That nigga is old school for real. He ain't no pimp or, player when it comes to women. The nigga is sharp." I just stood there peeping game, thinking how I was going to cut into him. This nigga had a mean streak within his demeanor and mannerism. It was written all over him. *I don't play,* and *don't try to play me if you want to live.* I knew that being cold and with skull game, was part of the code of being out here in this hell trying to find that black heaven that came with street notoriety and big money. "Spoons" was a street pharmacist. He stood 6' even with a slender dark mahogany frame complexion. He was a couple of years older than I was, and he dropped out of school." "Spoons" been hustling every since he was fourteen, due to his family ugly drug infested hood life. He had his own apartment. "Spoons" had three kids by three different women, and he came up in an orphan. His mother was killed from a trick that beat her to death, and his father was stabbed to death while doing time in the pen. His father was a street pharmacist also. The word on the street was that his old man owed a large some of money to a black syndicate that was twisted with an affiliation with the Italian syndicate, which was the reason for his death. When he got busted with two kilos and $170,000. He was sent up state to do 15 years, but he was murder fifteen days after his arrival. While standing in the chow line, he was stabbed 13 times before the guards was able to pull the killer off his father." Melody put her hands on both cheeks and her eyes just watered up. "Dad how can you or anybody live like that? I mean it's just so much killing, and horror for us as black people no matter what. It's like when you trying to do better it winds up bad, and when you are not doing anything, then you are still stuck in a bad situation also. I mean where is the middle line. I know that type of stuff happens out there, but when does it all ends?" Carlo "The Wiz' got up, and walked back over to the BBQ pit, and put the wings into the pan that was sitting on the pit's stand. His wife and daughter was talking among themselves about the horrors of street life. While Carlo "The Wiz" was taking the wings in the house, Mrs. Rodgers and her daughter came into the house to fix themselves a plate. After they all fix them something to eat, they went back outside. Just when Carlo "The Wiz" was about to sit down the phone ranged. He ran back into the house, but the phone stopped ringing before he could get it.

While on his way back out the door, the phone ranged again. It was his son-in-law on the line. He brought the cordless receiver to Melody, and after his son-in-law and him spoke to one another making small talk for a minute. He gave his daughter the phone. She was on the phone for a brief second. Her father asked her was everything alright. Her husband was just letting her know, that their son and him was at one of his co-worker's home having a few beers and talking. While the boys were inside playing video games."

Mrs. Rodgers went into the house, and came back with two small bottles of sweet red wine for her daughter and her. Mean while Carlo "The Wiz" continued to sip on his liquor, and roll up another stick of gangster-green. His wife asked him, "How can you drink that liquor in the middle of the day, hot as it is out here. Baby you going to pass out. Ha, ha" Carlo told her, "If I do pass out, you better pack my black ass into the house to cool off. That's why I brought this fan out here. Plus, it's cool sitting under this gazebo." She responded, "Yes, it does feel good." Melody stated, "Dad are you going to finish with your story?" Carlo "The Wiz" grinned a little responded, "Yes, baby-girl I am." Mrs. Rodgers, "There's that ole' devilish grin again." Carlo asked, "What are you talking about? You calling me a devil?" His wife replied, "You know I always said that grin just looks so mischievous. Because of your deep black well shaped eyebrows. You remember when we first met. I asked you did you arch your eyebrows. Melody your father almost had a fit, when I asked him that. Hell naw, I don't arched my eyebrows. What you calling me a faggot or pervert or something! Oh my God, that nigga was hot. Hah, ha!" Carlo commented, "Shit, my eyes were giving to me by God, to hypnotize your ass." His wife replied, "They sure were just for me, that's why I'm the wifey." She got up partially out her lounge chair, and gave her husband a little kiss. Carlo "The Wiz" stated, "Anyway Melody, the next time I went down to the club that's when I started rapping with Black Jack. It was a slow night not many people were in the club at the time. So, I walked over to Black Jack where he was sitting at the bar sipping on his drank. I said, "Black can I holler at you for second about something serious?" Black Jack shot, "About what lil nigga? I don't fuck with you youngsters, ya'll are too reckless and stuck on dumb stupid shit. You just keep it moving." His voice was so deep, it was as though the floor was vibrating when he spoke. I knew I had to come up with something that made me appear different than the average young cat running the streets. I came back like this, "I'm not like those young dumb niggas out here playing cowboys and Indians. I peeped game from the Old School from my father before he died." Black Jack asked, "Who is your Old Man?" I shot back with my chest stuck out, "Stomp Down!" Black Jack laughed. Then he stated, "Stomp Down is your Old Man? Damn, that was a hell of a nigga." Red the club owner stated, "He looks just like Stomp Down. Boy your Old Man was well respected out here. He always had some superfly women. When he met your mother, I knew his was going to change sooner or later. Now, that was a lady. Everybody tried to push upon her, but Stomp- Down had your mother on lock. He was old school alright. Gone Black, gone pull the lil nigga's coat. You see he's hungry for game. These lil' niggas think they hip already. Young Stomp Down coming to where it's at." Black Jack was staring me down without blinking his eyes, with a toothpick in his mouth. He said, "Lets step outside, and hibernate in my ride." We walked outside, and he popped the locks with his remote, and then we leaped in his black Caddy with gold trimming along with chrome rims. The windows were crystals clear. He turned the ignition, and the Caddy just roared, and then he turned the A/C on. It reminded me of when I would ride, and flip through the city with the Old Man. He removed his black homburg from his head, and ran his finger along the inner band. Then he retrieve a gangster green. He asked, "You smoke herb?" I told him that my father and I used to smoke together before he passed. He lit the gangster up, and looked over at me and said, "Lil' Stomp Down. Your Old Man and me used run together for a while. Then I burned off and went to the West-Coast. I've been back South about five years now. So Lil' Stomp what you want to talk with me about?" I replied, "I want to get my coat pulled to some serious game by a real season vet. Since my Old Man isn't here, and plus my Uncle Willie his brother died also." Black interrupted me. "That's right Ole'Slick Willie, they were brothers. Them brothers was doing there thing back in the days. Your Uncle Willie was a hell of a con man. That nigga was a smooth talking muthafucka, and your father was cold with the women. He wasn't no pimp, but people thought he was. But he wasn't, he just knew how to control women. Okay Lil' Stomp I'm pull your coat, and dress you up with some game, but don't make me regret taking you to school. This is some serious shit! Muthafuckas will kill, when you become too dangerous. What I mean about dangerous, is when you are too cleaver for them suckas, and you start shining, all the bitches want you, and then hating suckas will envy you and despise you. Our people will kill a muthafucka over stupid shit like envy of your game, and jealous because of what you have, you dig?" I told him, "I can dig it." Black Jack took me to school. I was focus and glued in like a cat seeking its next meal or prey. Black blasted, "Lil' Stomp, only damn fools wait, and the most stupid shit, I ever heard is niggas are waiting for a white blue eye Jesus to return. How in the hell can anyone wait for someone they have never seen before. See sharp niggas wait for what they can see, and knows what it looks like, and also what's coming. You want your game to be airtight, you dig?" I just shook my head. He continued, "You want your game to be so tight, with no room for cracks or leaks you dig? Like a bitch will go out there in that fucking danger, 100 degree weather, 20 below freezing and bring back her man all the money. Even the News on TV, it's a billion dollar propaganda machine. They will tell you some shit like, such and such dog ran away, and the family hasn't been able to find him. This and that is happening over seas, they called that news, how did that shit help anyone. See, out here niggas always got some news you can use, even if the shit has some gossip bullshit to it. It's still something that went down, going down, or about to go down. You need to listen to some of that shit, because when you out here, and that's part of survival to know what's going down, then you have to learn how to read a muthafucka. Now, when a hustler, player or season cat have serious game, he thinks like a hunter. You don't wait for shit, you be patience. Always be the hunter, never be the hunted, unless it's a bitch choosing you, can you dig it?" I asked, "Isn't that waiting?" Black looked at me with those cold red eyes, "Lil' nigga don't make me toss your little ass out my ride, asking some dumb shit like that. I just asked can you dig up what I am laying down." I said yes. Black went on, "No, because you are setting up shit to happen in your favor sooner or later. Remember what you setup has to unfold the way you set it up. When setting it up and it's fucked up, it's going to unfold fucked up, dig? Suckas wait for money from jobs and other bullshit, but hustlers set traps for rats to get his cheese. Everybody out here has to be a pawn for you, and you have to remain the king." Black Jack turned the radio up little, and "Hard Times" by the late great

Curtis Mayfield was playing smoothly. He was taking me to school. He was the street professor of tricknology and psychology. Then Black stated, "Lets slide to your pad." On the way to my pad, he stopped at the liquor store, and then he stopped at the rib shack. From there he stopped at the corner store. We were on our way to my pad. When we arrived, and went into the house. He sat down on the couch, and retrieved a pair of dice and a deck of cards. Then he stated, "Lil' Stomp bring me a glass of ice, a fork and roll that up." He threw a small bag of superb-herb at me to roll up. Then he passed me some chicken and ribs he got. After we finished smacking on them ribs and chicken. I was back in class. He said, "I'm teach you about the game of dice and vice, on cards and ghetto sharks, and the quick swap without a fatal drop." Black Jack ran down the game of psychology. "When you get inside another person's skull, you make damn sure you program that suckas' silicone wires to your data. It's like when it's raining cats and dogs, and the bitch will swerve in between those rain drops to make sure that her top-player get dry bread with big heads. That's what you have to do when you get down on these suckas, you dig? This game ain't for lames! Plus, I know you got heart, it's in your blood. The average black person are afraid to learn real game, that's why they steal, cheat, rob another black person that's living worse or on the same level they are. Real hustler hustle the able, which is them squares with Victorian dinning tables, you dig? Just like God tried to shield Job from Satan. You can't stop a muthafucka from getting what they suppose to be having. That's why God took that shield off Job, so he could see the worst to grow, and recognize the good and best when he gets it. You got to go thorough some shit. Let me pull your coat to some real game, that real players studied, and applied that same shit to their game. It's all psychological, in other words. It's called skull game, baby. Getting them suckas to love losing, and losing and loving it the same time, while they give you their winnings. They call it killing them softly, can you dig it? Everyday in America wherever there is a casino, suckas are taking their hard earn money to the casino, which is established and setup to break their dumb lame asses. Day and night 24/7 them suckas and lames giving their money away on a thrill, on a hope, on a wish, hell some of them even pray for a winning. When that sucka prays he becomes a bigger sucka, because now he thinks God is his on his side. What does he do, he keeps gambling like a damn fool. Then, when he's broke that's when he gets to see how big of fool he really is. The real players and hustlers peep game, and learn the lesson for him to be like the casinos, and set up something that's going to keep his pockets fat. In order to learn how to win, and become a better player you have to accept your losses, and look into the reasons you keep losing. You going to loose sometime, but you want to make it where you cut the risk, dig? As long as you keep losing, that means you are not a sharp hustler, you dig? Every move you make is to set up another play to win. Man, Old Stomp Down that was a no non-sense muthafucka there. Kid it's in your blood to be a top-notch player or a real hustler." I was pulling on that gangster, while Black was pulling my coat, and he was steady sipping on the cognac. I could tell that my Old Man made an impression on Black and the other street cats that knew him. He told me, "I want you to learn how to take these small dice, and learn to talk with them in your mouth, that way you can learn to blow on the dice, and make the switch, without it being noticeable. You have to learn how to talk with them in your mouth in order for you to make the smooth switch." He pulled another pair of dice out, and every time he threw them he rolled a seven or eleven back to back. He showed me that he had the dice filed down just a little where it was hard to tell unless you looked closely. Then he pulled out a deck of cards, and dealt us each hand of five cards. I had a good hand, then he asked, "You have a good hand, huh?" I told him that I did. Black said, "You know how I know you have a good hand. You got too excited. Lil' Stomp, you can never get too excited out here about nothing. That's a sign of a boy's minds and it tells cats you are green. Always look serious and talk serious. Your father was a non–sense type of cat. He was always like a block of ice sitting on ice cream. Cold and sweet, and women couldn't resist him, and street cats always saw his cold side. When you are cold, nobody knows how to read you or size you up, dig. I'm deal another hand." He looked at me again, "You got a good hand again right?' I did, Black, stated, "This time I was able to read you by the vein on the side of your neck. You didn't show it on your face, but you were still revealing what I was able to read. That's what you don't want. When suckas see they can move you, that's a sign of weakness. Ok, lets play another hand." He dealt us another hand,' Black said, "You got a fucked up hand this time." I shook my head yes. Black stated, "You frowned a little which is what?" I replied, "I have bad hand, and I made it known." Black told me, "Remember to keep all your emotions to yourself, unless you have to use them to set up the shit you trying to set up. Mainly, that's when a bitch is involved, but to a certain degree. You let her know that she can't move you emotionally too much either. Now, she has to see some emotional acts from you, which shows her that you are passionate or have some regards concerning her. Sometimes you have to act like you got a fucked up hand, but really you have a winning hand. At other times you have to act like you got a good hand, but it's fucked up hand. That makes the sucka give in quickly, or throw the game. Alright that's enough for the night, lets split the scene."

"We jumped back into Black Jack's Caddy, and headed back to the club. While on the way to the club I still had those dice in my mouth. The club appeared to be jumping from all the cars that was parked in front of the club. And along the side of the street. Black Jack pulled up close to the club, and turned the ride off. We just sat there for a moment. Black said, "Kid I'm turn you on to Flip. We used to run together, but Flip got hooked on them drugs, but the nigga still sharp. He fucks with that shit, but he always keeps a ride, and money in his pocket. He just fucks with that shit too much. It's taking him down slowly. Flip was a cold nigga out her kid. Even some of the sharpest cats think they are invincible or they think they can fuck with that shit without repercussions, but they all found out the hard way. That dog-food don't give a damn about no one, you hear me, no one! Don't ever fuck with that shit whether getting paid or smoking. They are giving niggas time that ain't worth fucking with that shit. I smoke my herb, sip my yak and hustle for my bread. Don't forget what I'm rapping. I'll be checking in with you from time to time. Kid, I pulled your coat to some serious game, like being on deck of a big beautiful yacht riding the waves of the seas of life, but there's a lot more to this game. So just let that shit I hip you to, dress your skull and hip you to the code of playing, you dig?" When I spit those dice out of my mouth. Black was like kid, "You still had those dice in your jib?" I responded, "For sure." We both laughed, and he gave me some dab. Black said, "Kid I knew you had it in you." Black said, "Keep practicing. The better you will be, you dig?" He looked at me with that deep cold- hard look. " I told Black that he did, then we hopped out of his Caddy and swagger on into the club. With all that I had soaked up, I felt like a high-powered player that was ready to make some fucking serious moves. Remembering what Black said, be patience, and think and move like a hunter. Melody asked, "Dad, how did you use that to get where you are now?" Carlo "The Wiz" replied, "In order for me to get close to the big money makers or get to the point of getting serious money. I had to look like money, think like top-players. Real players wear their outfits according to the game they all are playing. Big bankers wear expensive suits, and cops wear their uniforms. So every profession or players have a dress code, dig? The main thing I had to do was remain on top of the deck, and deal a few of my cards from the bottom of the deck after the shuffle, without the person I was playing against noticing it or able to peep my game."

Singing The Blues

Carlo "The Wiz" and his family were still sitting out back enjoying each others company and time together. In the hood it's an everyday thing to congregate together, but unfortunately sometimes these family gatherings leads to a fight, arguments or some server physical injuries. Not everyone understands the value and blood connections of loyalty to the family unit. Today, the family unit appears to be breaking down like tumor cells, that breaks away from the good cell unit, and become bad cells within the body. Also with families and people, the breakage from good family unit to bad family unit leads to a tumor within the family unit, and if it goes untreated without love, respect and loyalty it becomes a deadly cancer among the family, especially when money is involved. Everything Carlo "The Wiz" did was for him to become a rich nigga. The plans, tactics and strategies were calculated for the greater good. Carlo leaned over, and retrieved the bottle of liquor, and poured himself another drink. He got up, and went over to the built in bar, and retrieved the ice tray and shook a few cubes into his glass of imported liquor. Melody got up and went into the house to use the bathroom. Mrs. Rodgers looked at her husband

and stated, "Honey, you think she's handling all this, okay? A few times she was almost crying. Did you see that?" Carlo gave a little sigh and replied, "Yes, I saw that. She can handle it. Plus, it's just a sign of her pure innocence of not being tainted and her sadness is the reality that she never have to face or encounter these types of life threaten situations. What I'm convening to her, is to never think for a minute about venturing down in the concrete jungle, without knowing the horrors that's been heaped upon us as a people. When my grand-son become of age, I'm going to tell him about the horrors of the street life, before he has a taste of street venom within his veins. See baby, whenever you get some street venom in your veins, you have to get another anti-venom to override the first bite, you dig?" She asked, "What's the second bite?" Carlo "The Wiz" told his wife, "Whenever something really tragic happens to you out there, and you make it. You rarely go back, and if you do go back. You tell yourself this is not going to happen again, but it does happen again, and sometimes much worse. The first tragedy is the warning, unfortunately many of us don't heed the warning, we call it being true to the hood. That's like saying I'm true to killing my own people or living with a grenade stuck up my ass, and just waiting for some muthafucka to pull the pin. But how many of us knock off the ones that's killing us all. When Melody walked up her father was finishing his statement. She was feeling at little tipsy and asked, "What are you two love birds talking about?" Her mother told her they were talking about the horrors, tragedy and deaths when comes to living the street life. Melody commented, "It's just so sad how we treat one another day in and day out. The saddest part is we don't want anybody to hurt our families, but being true is hurting someone else's family. It's just stupid and crazy.

It doesn't make any sense. Anyway, go ahead father, and finish telling the story. It's very interesting and sad also."

Carlo "The Wiz" continued, "I got dress this morning, and called a cab, because I sold my father's car. The bus and cab was my means of getting around for the most part." Melody asked her father, "How much did you get for the car? He stated $8000, then he began telling his story again. "When the cab pulled up in front of the house, I jumped in and the cab driver torpedo away from the driveway. We were headed down to Windy Street and Blacksmith Street. That's where cats would hang out on the block. The liquor store was on the block, and also the QQG store was next to the liquor store. Walking to where the street cats were standing. I looked around and saw Flip at the QQG store. So I ran across the street. He was coming out of the store when I spoke to him. I said, "What's happen Flip?" He replied, "Do I know you?" I told him, "Not really, but Black Jack told me to holler you about something. In other words I'm ready to go to school." Flip leaned up against his white Cadillac Brougham, and responded," I really don't fuck with you lil' niggas. Ya'll bring to much heat to a brother. You muthafuckas don't listen, and ya'll too hot headed. I got a good thing going for myself, and don't live that lifestyle no more. I'm too old for fun and games." We both hopped in his Hog, and burned out. Flip was a very thin cat. He was so thin you could probably push him down with one finger. Flip was a down cat, and he smelled as though he missed one or two days of showering his thin frame. He had some black dress bottoms, black loafers with snake skin on top, white button dress silk shirt, and a gold watch and picky ring on left hand and wrist. His hair was slicked back in shabby ponytail. Flip commented, "Now, I got much love for that nigga Black. That's my nigga on the real. I don't know why he want me to holler at you, and what about. I don't know! Plus, who are your peeps?" I told him that Stomp-Down was my Old Man. Flip said, " Oh, that's why! Youngblood, Black calls you Lil' Stomp, right?" I told him, "Yep, that's what they called my Old Man." Flip cracked, "I didn't know him personally, like I know Black Jack, but I knew of him. Your Old Man and Black are much older than me. Black and I hooked up years later, when I was coming up. So you are ready for school?" I responded that I was ready. Flip bellowed, "That's what makes the world go around. Those that want to got to school, those that are forced to go, and those that never go to school. Which has become the way of the present world. What I mean is, you what to know, while stupid suckas think they already know what's happening out here, and get caught up doing life in the pen. When you go to school you eliminate some of the bullshit that's unnecessary. But them stupid suckas, and lames feel it's necessary. As the saying goes a hard head learns the hard way, and that's the only way they can learn. That can be very costly, and plus, that's the only way a hard head can learn, which is the hard way. It all boils down to what you are doing, why you are doing it, how you are doing it, and where you are doing at. You get my meaning?" We were flipping through the city from the Southwest side to the North side, when I told him that I understood. Flip continued, "I did time for petty theft. I snatched a lady's purse, and ran around the corner. When I hit that corner, ha, ha…that damn Roller was sitting right at the corner. Plus, that bitch was running behind me. I did 90 days in the county for that bullshit, ha, ha…man that shit is funny just thinking about it." I asked Flip, Why did you snatch the lady purse?" Flip bellowed, "Man, when you got a drug addict mother, and a father doing life in the pen for shooting Rollers, during a bank robbery. You have to do what it takes to survive. I remember when I was coming up, my mother would just ride my father about finding himself a job. Jobs were hard to come by at that time, shit even today! My father would tell her all the time, that he couldn't make no one hire him. I think that's what drove my father to rob that bank that day. He was trying to provide for his family. I think he just cracked, with the attitude with fuck it! See, that's the thing that you youngsters don't seem to get. We old cats made them mistakes for ya'll, but ya'll go right back out there, and do the same stupid shit, thinking ya'll are slicker. What them youngsters fail to get is, whenever you commit some type of crime. The Rollers become a little more strategic of that crime, because the city puts the heat on the mayor, then the mayor put pressure on the police chief. Then, chief puts the pressure on the sheriff, and the sheriff rips the deputies a new ass hole. The legislature puts new law into effect concerning that crime, and judicial people makes a judgment on how it will benefit their stocks and investments concerning the prison industrial system, and finally the executive branch sets the time a person will get for that crime if he's black versus the time a white person will get for the same crime. That's a bum hustle snatching purses! Some of those women that have expensive purses on their shoulder are broke, but they dress like they have a million dollars. And the only way you going to know if they got money in them purses is by getting that muthafucking purse. Them lame bitches be broker than two hobos and a dope fiend." We both laughed. I thought this nigga was a clown, and a bullshitter. But the more I listened to him he was right on. Flip pulled me back into the classroom, "Lil' Stomp, I don't claim to be a hell of a player, but in this war zone called the hood. You better think like a solider, a general, a captain and most of all like a strategic player in this game call life. See, I would find myself looking for a woman that wanted something out of life, or women just enjoyed me like funk on shit. Whenever the chic got used to me being around her, that's when I would disappear. It made her wonder, or long for me to be back within her circle. When I would pop back on the scene again, I would tell her a story about the money and big money moves and flash a roll, you dig? That would reinforce what I say, and show what I putting down on her. That's called imagery impressions. I really don't trust women, and that's why I don't really get too involve with them emotionally, at least not back then. Whenever they would reveal their love and deep attachment, I would back off. This would make them plead to get close to me, and I would do that to make her die to be involve with me even if it meant for her to do the unthinkable. The thing she wants the most or desired, I used that desire as my tool and bait. I would move them to my point of reasoning and money schemes. In essence they make themselves willing pawns. Out in this rat infested hood today niggas want notoriety and fame, some want money, some want a sense of power, and the other kittens don't know what to do with themselves so they just follow whomever. Today it's all about fame, big egos and material shit, but back in my day it was about survival shit. You don't want to shine too much out here, because these envious and hating ass niggas will put your lights out. Lil' Stomp always know where the light switch or power is, so when you see fit to turn them fucking lights off, you got to turn them fucking lights off. Can you dig up what I'm putting down?" I replied, "I dig it." Flip took me back to school, "Like a said before, I'm no woman's man, but I learned the hard way on why I had to sharpen up my game. I'm crack this game on how I got some of my skills to deal with scandalous ass bitches. I think I was fifteen or sixteen years old when I was kicking it with this older bitch. This chic was twenty-five years older than me. But I got word from Freaky D. We were shooting the shit one night, and he cracked that the bitch was a freak for young studs. That bitch had me wrapped around her fucking finger, and plus she was married. I was green as a pool table top, and square as a box of cigarettes. I was on a fucking high while fucking with this old bitch, and I thought I was the shit. The bitch would call me whenever her husband went to work, and I would bring over some herb and blow. After smoking and rubbing them big soft helium blown thighs. I was ready to jump into the sack with this bitch. The bitch detoured on my conquest, and just started playing, teasing and toying with my muthafucking ass. After getting my nose froze, and trying to imitate them real no-nonsense players. I slapped the bitch so hard I hurt my fucking hand, and the bitch flipped off the couch and hit the fucking floor. I was yelling at that bitch, who do you think you fucking with? The bitch was begging me not to hit her again. I kicked that bitch in her fucking side, and just went to kicking the bitch. I didn't hear the bitch make a sound or show some sign of resistance like before. When I stopped I checked to see if the bitch was still breathing. She was still breathing. I made a quick dash like a slave running for freedom. Hours later them Rollers was slapping them steel bracelets on my wrist. I had to do five years in the state penitentiary on assault and battery, and plus criminal trespass. Listen to me carefully Lil' Stomp, life in the pen is no fucking joke! Whenever you got 90% of angry niggas in one spot, you got total mayhem and chaos. Some of them are locked up because of their skin color, being at the wrong place at the wrong time, associated with the wrongs cats, and trying to make a living which forces some us to do things they call crime. We all know that slavery is a crime, so they created laws to justify the causes and reason for slavery. Life in the pen is a everyday confrontation with death. That's a helluva life to live. Facing death everyday until you get release, if you are able to live through the death traps inside. Some niggas, whether black, white or Latino will release their sexual pressure by sodomizing other men. Then, you should dig why they call it the penal system. It's another word for penis. This system is out to fuck every black person in this country, and Hispanics also. When you got faggots running the system, then they create laws, systems and situation to fuck you, which pleases their sexual fucked up cravings and desires. When I got caught up I told myself, I will never get locked down behind a trifling bitch again. I knew I had to sharpen my game, you dig? I learned the art of psychological skullduggery." I interjected, "What's psychological skullduggery?" Flip replied, "I'm glad you asked. It's the art of psychological trickery, from politics to economical control. I get the women hooked on being with me like a fish on a hook, and then pull a Houdini and split the scene. When it comes to running game on them, you play them close and then you back up."

As Carlo "The Wiz" was moving his lips, and the sun also was making its move towards the south. It wasn't near dark, but the heat of the light was becoming intensified. Melody asked, "So father what happened next?" Carlo stated, "We stopped at the Barber shop. Flip got a edge up, and clean hot towel shave. He reached in his front pocket of his shirt, while we were perched in front of the barber shop in his ride. He pulled out a small zip-lock of white candy, and some gangster from a match box, and shook some candy into the slight folded 1-1/4 paper and herb. He looked at me coldly and said with a gripped whisper, "Don't you ever do this shit! I started doing this shit while fucking with that same bitch I just told you about. I'm say this and then I'm have to bury the seed with you until a later time. I make $40,000 a year. I have a gig at the Elite restaurant. I am manager there, I have a nice town home, and nice Latino chic, that's been down with me like a roots to a tree. Dig this Lil' Stomp, The game was once beautiful, it's ugly and upside down, and every nigga you see in the hood has written on their faces either game or a frown." He dropped me off at the Foxx Inn Lounge on Sixth and Broadway. It was only few cars parked out front. We said our fair wells until the next time. I was down for mine. The more game I got the slicker I was feeling, but I couldn't let that over ride the reality, that I was still green and unseasoned. I couldn't stop, which that would mean that all this planning was for nothing. I limped into the Lounge with a cool swagger, and when I hit the door. The late great Bobby "Blue" Bland was blasting heavy truth and game from the joke-box on the life in the city among us soul drenched niggas. It became on of my favorite songs, 'Ain't No Love In The Heart of the City.' My father would play that song all the time. I copped me a coke, and took a seat at a booth in the back. Soaking up all the shit Flip cracked on me. Like I said, I was feeling some type of slickness about myself. I was sitting there contemplating my next move." The phone started ringing again, but no one moved to answer it. Meoldy, her mother and father sat there for a moment before anyone said anything. They were enjoying each others company and love, which today very few black families can do unconditionally. Many of them will express their love verbally, but when it came down to showing it, it's a blank check that can never be cashed.

Putting Down Game

Carlo "The Wiz's" story was getting deeper as time rolled on. Mrs. Rodgers looked at her husband and knew he was getting very intoxicated as he was revealing his story of success to his beautiful daughter. Carlo didn't like telling stories like this at times, because the young took stories like this as bragging or boasting. Which many of today's youngsters missed the point of what game is, and what it truly means to have game. Mrs. Rodgers asked her husband, "Baby are you drunk? You are going to finish this story, right. Your baby-girl and I have been following you whole heartily with this story. So, you can't stop now. Don't you leave us hanging, and wondering how you made all this possible." Carlo "The Wiz" laughed and responded, "Baby have I ever left you hanging?" Mrs. Rodgers looked at her husband, and twisted her lips at him, and turned her head a little, and made huh... sound. Then she replied, "It was a few times you left mc hanging when we first started messing around. Man, I used to hate whenever you did that. I just couldn't wait to see you again, and put my hands around your neck and just shake you." Little did she know she was just reinforcing what Carlo "The Wiz" did to win her, which was to put his game around her soul, just as much she wanted to put her hands around his neck to choke and shake him for pushing and pulling on her deep emotions. "Okay baby I'm finish telling my ladies the story. Anyway, my money was getting a little low with the one family rental home I was renting to this middle age family, which helped me stay a float for a while. But I was till getting pink slip after pink slip in the mail. And the middle-aged family helped me stayed longer than I anticipated, but that was good for me. It worked out the way I needed it. That way I can keep enough money in the bank to show the bankers that I am able to control my finances, which later they offered me a loan. That's when I went searching for another rental property. But my whole plan was to move up the ladder, and get those corporate connections. One night when I was walking to the "Pink Pony Club." I had called the cab company, but the cab was taking too long, and the city bus stops running after 9pm. I just started walking. When I came to Windy and Blacksmith Street. I went into the QQG to cop me some suds." Melody asked her father, "Suds, what is suds?" Carlo responded with a little humor, "A beer greenie." He didn't like that his daughter was that green, but on the flip side, he did. I guess it goes to show, you can't always have shit the way you totally like for it to be, but that's life. That's one of the main reasons he didn't mind telling stories like this to young kids, and his daughter. Most cats always told stories with hype, and not the dark side they keep out of sight. Many cats told stories to stroke their egos, while the old school broke down game with the A-side and the B-side, they knew you couldn't have one without the other. Carlo "The Wiz" went on, "While walking inside the store, this dude and I just bumped into each other. I wasn't trying to bump into him, and I didn't know if he did it intentionally to me. I threw up my hands, telling him everything was cool. When I had my hands up like this."

Carlo "The Wiz" got up to demonstrate how he had his hands up for his daughter. Then, he continued, " I had my hands up like so if he threw a punch, I would be able to block his blow. And that's exactly what he did. He swung, and missed I pushed him into a parked car, which made him lose his balance. That's when I hit him, and then he fell. I just went to kicking and kicking that guy. Then I ran off. He was still laying there. When I was running, I passed Black Jack . He slammed on his brakes, and put the car in reverse. I hopped in, and we burned off. We rode over to the Foxx Inn Lounge. Black asked me what was going on. I told him that I just had a fight. Black asked, "Did you beat his ass?" I stated, "Hell yes!" Black shot back, "Then you good. You beat his ass good enough to put some fear in him, or at least enough for him not to fuck with you again. If you did that, then you did good. He wont come back for more. Where did it go down?" I responded, "At the QQG." Black said, "Lets roll by there to see what's happening." As we rolled by the QQG the patty wagon was putting the guy in the ambulance, and the Rollers were asking questions. We all know that real niggas don't crack or snitch. We rolled on to our destination, which was the Foxx Inn Lounge. I told Black, "I'm trying to stay out of trouble, because of what I trying to do. I don't want a rap sheet, that's one good reason they need to bar a nigga from getting into that corporate game." Black Jack shot back, "Dummy up Lil' Stomp. The day you were born, you and every nigga that ever was born, was barred from that corporate world. They have placed us in cells where the bars are invisible, but they are there! Every real nigga out here know them bars are around us. Them bourgeoisie niggas know it too. They just choose to kiss whitey's ass and lick his balls to be in that game. Them no good muthafucking peckerwoods think we are some dumb jiving ass niggas, that doesn't mean nobody any good. It least that's what they tell the world, but they know different. Because the superior wouldn't waste time kicking, beating and strategizing to keep the blind, deaf and ignorant in there so-called place. The losers and the confused know their place. So that's why they do what they do, because they know we are some muthafuckas. Would you waste your time on a loser, if that's what you consider that person or people to be?" I popped, "Hell no! That's stupid shit." Black continue, "Not even God, gives a fuck about us. That's why he cursed us. That's what the white folks believe, and they believe that shit as sure as my ass is black and my eyes are blood shot. So, you get this into that skull of yours, being on these streets it's called the University of the Concrete Jungle. You are exposed to all types of shit. I mean you have to really be on your game out here. Real hustlers are inside that corporate world you are rapping about, because that's where making big money is and all about, and they learned the game of the corporate seats. We call it corporate pimping or corporate players. That's when a nigga go from the streets to the corporate seats. And some of those cats have rap sheets as long as Interstate-10 you dig? The game is all about money. America was built on material wealth. That's all you see on the TV screens, is material shit." When we pulled up in front of the Lounge. Black said, "I got another card trick I need to show you, but you got to be careful. In the mean time, I want you to rap with "Cat Daddy." That's another nigga I think you can get some game from, and plus that nigga is cool, and he can be a little beside himself. But fuck that! Get what you can use, and then blow a fuse. "Cat Daddy" got laced by "Mr. Sinclair." And that nigga got laced by "Too Clean," I am talking to you about some serious game that go way back, you dig? Now "Cat Daddy" is little younger than I am, but older than you. Mr. Sinclair is about seventy-seven, or something like that. The nigga is old school all the way, and not because of his age, but because of his ways and what he got from the old school. This place right here, is one of Mr. Sinclair's place. The nigga is stuffed with cash, but he's not flashy about it. It's about staying under the radar, you dig? When you stand out it's not because of your flash, it's because of your demeanor. Your realness will always stand out, if you are true to being who you are, other than that what you will be labeled a funky-flunkey, basically a square-bitch ass nigga, you dig? If you got heart, brains and some big balls you will make it to that place in your skull you keep creating. That's where it all game begins baby, that's where all game is played. Remember this, it's all skull game, you dig?" While Black was telling me this he was pointing to his skull. Then, he stated, "Lets go in here, and have a few bottles of suds." We hopped out of the Caddy, and limped on in. That was the first time that I ever been in the Foxx Inn Lounge. While we were sitting at the bar sipping on some suds. Minutes later the door opened, and the tall figure of guy walked in with a lady that had style and grace as she moved about. Behind the both of the two towering figures was a young graceful looking stud. They walked over to the bar and spoke to the lady and man bartender. Next, the tall suave giant and Black Jack gave each other some dap, and the lady gave Black Jack a hug. Black and the young looking stud shook hands. This towering of a figure asked Black, "Who is the young-buck you have with you?" Black Jack replied, "That's Lil' Stomp Down!" The man that asked and stepped back and bellowed, "What! Are you serious? This Stomp Down's son. Damn! Boy your Old Man was a son-of-a-bitch. He didn't take no shit off nobody. We going have to sit down, and talk one day. I owe that much to you because of your father." Black Jack interjected, " That's why I brought him by." The suave fellow, that carried himself like a king, "Good, let me take care of some business, and catch up with you and Lil' Stomp a little later." Black Jack, "That's groovy Mr. Sinclair." Mr. Sinclair lead and, the lady and the young stud followed the King Mr. Sinclair through a door that read 'Private Personal Only.' I asked, "That's the Mr. Sinclair everyone talks about?" Black replied, "The one and only. That's one sharp cat, plus the young stud helps run this joint." I asked, "Who is the young stud?" Black took a sip of beer, and in his slow deep baritone voice, "That's Cat-Daddy. Mr. Sinclair pulled Cat-Daddy's coat. Plus, Cat-Daddy, is much younger than your Old Man, and me. Mr. Sinclair is about seventy-five or seventy. I know he's in his seventies." After spinning around on the stool at the bar, and looking at the door the threesome went through, I asked, "Who is the lady that's with them?" Black looked over his right shoulder where I was sitting next to him at the bar commented, "That's Mrs. Sinclair's wife. They been together every since Mr. Sinclair was in the game. She's a die hard down lady too. She's originally from the Big Easy. They used to call her, huh Madame Divine and some still do call her Madame Divine. They said she knew how to work that Black Magic on muthafuckas." I was spell bound. I was thinking did she hook Mr. Sinclair by using that Black Magic or did Mr. Sinclair hook her with game and wits, or maybe it's just a match that had to happen no matter what the situation was. I guess when we get a chance to rap, I'll get the scoop probably. Mr. Sinclair and Cat Daddy were two down cats I had to get my coat pulled by. Even if I had to ride a bicycle without tubes and tires, or drive a car with three flat tires with two spare inner tubes, I needed that game. Hell, even if I had to ride the wrong train, on the right track, I had to get there or no matter the transportation. It was a muthafucking must!" Carlo's wife and daughter cracked on his last statement about his means of transportation to get where he desired to be at all cost. That's one thing Mrs. Rodgers understood and knew greatly went it came to her husband's determination. Once he had a vision, nothing could detour him from that vision that he felt or saw a little light at the end of the tunnel.

"After sipping on two beers, and retrieving a third, and I wasn't twenty-one yet. One thing we all know coming up in the hood, is there are many facets of life that has forced many of us to grow up fast. Our age and looks never coincides. Everyday hood struggles can, and will take a toll on anyone that endure economical struggles, family breakdowns, unemployment, drug addiction, alcoholism, police brutality, false conviction, serving or during time for someone's else crime, being framed due to the lack of evidence or failure of due process in those kangaroo courts called justice, and hopeless depression which leads to many vices and destructive devices, called ghetto coping. While Black Jack and I were sitting at the bar talking, Cat-Daddy walked up, and told me, "Lets go up to the VIP section and rap. And Ms. Louise can you bring us a bottle of scotch and bucket of ice to the VIP section, when you get a chance?" Then he pulled out his bank roll, and threw a crisp one-hundred dollar bill on the bar, and told her, "Keep the change." Carlo "The Wiz" went on with his story, "I followed Cat Daddy up a few steps. His vines were on point, red and white pin stripe suit, white tie, with white handkerchief bulging out his left upper pocket. He had on a large diamond pinky ring on each pinky finger, a gold watch, a diamond earring in his right-ear. He also had on red and white lid, that was cocked ace-duce, with a small white feather on the left side. His shoes was glossing red and white gator with a gold buckle on both shoes. He walked with a limp that said I'm hip, fly and rich. When we got up the few steps, we made a right turn. There was a long leather couch that was shaped in the letter C. There was a small table with ashtrays at the end of both sides of the black leather couch. The neon light was hitting his diamonds that made it bling and ting. When we finally sat down to talk, that cat opened up his volume of game, one of his ivory spikes, was dressed with a solitaire diamond, with a gold trimming. This cat really made an impression on me. That made it official to stick to my plans, like a nipple on a bitch's tits. It was still early in the night, and down the few steps was a long stage, with two shiny stainless steel poles on the stage. I knew what they were for, but no women or dancers had arrive at that time. Well black people never come to anything early, we always save the best for last, or time was something we just never considered strongly. So, while sitting there the female bartender brought the drink and the bucket of ice. Cat-Daddy lit a stick of gangster, and dropped a few ice cubes into the glass. Next, he poured himself a drink, and passed me the gangster. Before I took a pull, I had already prepared my drink. I was greatly ready for this cat to drop some game on me. It seems as though the more I wanted it the longer it took. I was thinking maybe he was sizing me up to see, if I'm a square, a lame or did I really have some player bones in my body." Melody responded, "Wow." Carlo asked his daughter, "What you mean baby-girl, by wow?" Melody shook her head and then replied, "That doesn't sound like you. I know you lost your father early, that guy and the others were like your father figures. You seem so more knowledgeable, than what I hearing." Carlo "The Wiz" responded, "That's only because I took what I was taught on the streets a little further than the average cat. The average cat doesn't read books, he thinks that books are useless. For some cats books are useless, until that knowledge becomes a life saver or strategy tool. Only then will books be useful. See momma would always read. I didn't see dad read much, but he would at time read the newspaper and the bible. That's after he stop living the life." Mrs. Rodgers interjected, "Your father is a Gemini, and you know what they say about Geminis. Two people in one, with crazy unpredictable ways of life." They all laughed. Mrs. Rodgers told her husband, "Go ahead baby. I didn't mean to cut you off." She lend over in her chair and gave her husband a slow passionate kiss again. Melody was like, "Mmm, you love birds want me to leave?" Carlo got up and started hugging and kissing his daughter tightly in a playful manner. Mrs. Rodgers just loved that side of her husband. He was passionate, and sometimes down right harsh and ruthless. She understood that was just who he had to be in order to make it in life with no one by his side. No brother, no sister, no cousins and no uncle and no aunt. The little family that he had were all dead and gone. He was smart, intelligent, caring, ambitious, devoted and well respected. Carlo "The Wiz" went back into the house, and grabbed a chicken leg. He was suffering from the munches, due to that superb-herb. He sat back down, and poured himself another drink. Carlo "The Wiz', said, "Were was I, Okay. Cat daddy asked me, "Where do you see yourself in the next five to ten years?" Without hesitation I replied, "I will be a millionaire! Living that life I am destine to live by all means." Cat Daddy shot back with an iron-cast stare, "What's your plan to make it happen? A lot of suckas wish, hope and dream to be rich or have some major bread, very few of them do anything. What makes you so different from the rest of them suckas?" I knew the test was coming, so I responded with an angle not to come off too cocky, "If I didn't have a major plan to put into effect, I wouldn't have wasted Black Jack's time. To make it all groovy and on the level I know he's hip and crafty enough to see through all kinds of bullshit." Cat-Daddy responded, "I knew you were going to drag Black through your lame ass grit. We will see how much game you really got! You can bullshit Black, because your Old Man and him was tight. I heard about your Old Man, and ran into him a few times. Plus, he sold game like a player suppose to. You down here trying to get your coat pulled by season players and hustlers, like every other sucka wishing to get hip to game. In a few tic and tocks this joint going to be loaded with felines, my headlights going be glued to your lame ass. You dig where I'm coming from?" I popped, "I'm hip to where you coming from. In the process don't let them wires cause your headlights to go out or too dim to see the game headed your way." Melody asked, "Dad were you a little angry, from the way he was coming at you?" Melody's mother interjected, "I thought the same thing. From the responds you gave him. You said at first that you wasn't trying to come off too strong, and if you did you probably wasn't going to get the information you were trying to get." Carlo "The Wiz" was like, "Hell yes, I got heated! I knew what he was trying to do. Not only was he trying to see if I can pick up game, but do I have enough balls to put it down." Mrs. Rodgers stated, "Go ahead baby, we just keep interrupting you." Carlo "The Wiz", "You want to hear the story but you and sweet baby-girl keep interrupting." Mrs. Rodgers' words filled with great passion, "Honey I am just trying to understand what you are saying, and what you went through. That's why your baby-girl and I ask questions when you tell us something we don't really understand. As you would say, can you dig it? We aren't from that life. We know it's harsh, and for some of our people it's a means of survival. That's all baby…you understand. Love you too. And baby what happen to the guy you had the fight with the corner store that night. You said the patty-wagon came to get him?" Carlo "The Wiz," "You know I love both of you very much. Anyway, that guy just got had his mouth wired that's all. He was a soup sucking muthafucka. While sitting there with Cat-Daddy drinking, and smoking no one said nothing for a moment. Suddenly, the front door flew open, and a stampede of sexy women burst through. It was about six women, and four trailed behind them. I looked over at Cat-Daddy, and he was looking right at me. I knew he was trying see my reaction. He was sitting there with his legs crossed, and hands crossed on his thigh. Two sexy through-breds came up the short steps to the VIP section. They spoke to Cat-Daddy, "Hey, daddy."

Cat-Daddy stated, "How are you ladies feeling tonight. I want you ladies to meet huh…huh…want they call you again?" I knew the nigga was fronting on me. I rolled, they call me Lil' Stomp Down. Your names? One of the women standing tall like a through-bred horse responded, they call me Delicious, and this is my friend. Her name is Sweet-Cakes. Both women stood about five feet and 9 inches tall. They were slightly tall women with large round hips and butt checks that looked like two half moons on each lady, with shapely thighs. Shit, plus I was focusing on their necks to see if they had a Adam's Apple. These were some, somewhat tall women. Nature doesn't produce very tall women, on the average most women are shorter than average man's height. But most guys don't pay attention, because they don't know that." Carlo closed his eyes when he was describing the women to his wife and daughter. His wife stated, "You surc remember that very well!" Carlo "The Wiz" replied, "Damn baby, why you acting insecure? We wasn't together yet ." She stated, "So it doesn't matter! It's the way you told that part of the story, and your bodily actions. Like you were living it all over again. Ask Melody what your demeanor was saying. It was like you were enjoying those women bodies.

Why were they your women then?" Carlo "The Wiz" shot back, "It was a topless joint. That's their job. I learned later, that a few of them women were dancing to pay their way through college, and the other few knew that it was good money in it." Melody stated, " I heard one of my classmate talking about the money she was making, but her boyfriend and her had to split because he didn't like for her to work in that type of environment." Carlo "The Wiz," "Yes, a lot of the young fellows are very insecure about things like that. Their feelings usually crack under pressure like this. That's why experience and confidence of knowing who you are is very important to one's survival and mental stability, you dig? So, why I'm sitting there, and being half-ass introduced. One of the women that was..." Mrs. Rogers interrupted, "I don't want to hear anything about you, and them women!" Carlo "The Wiz" cracked, "Are you fucking serious? You tripping on some shit that happened years ago. You wanted to hear the story, now you can't get past some shit that happened years ago. Go in the fucking house then, and baby-girl and I will sit out here and finish rapping!" Carlo knew within his heart he could never admit to his wife that he partook with a few women at the strip club when the opportunity presented itself. Plus, he knew that some things are to never be admitted, because normal people and lames condemn what they fail or couldn't understand. So, to remain clean and good in his wife's eyes he stuck to the script, and remain the way she needed and wanted to see her husband, a honest, clean and serious hustlers with goals. What most young cats coming up in the game fail to understand is that some things you have to take to the grave with you, other than your scars. Because a dead man can't explain or defend his motive or his causes of action. Mrs. Rodgers got up and jetted from the scene, and darted into the house. Melody asked her father, "Dad what's wrong with mom? I mean, I have never seen her act like this!" Carlo told his daughter, "I think your mother going back to when we had our ups and downs. She probably think those women were the cause but they weren't. Those ladies worked for that business, which was strictly business. They were off limits during business hours. I never locked-up with any those women. My focus was getting knowledge on the game. My father was a street wise cat, and seeing how he used it and conducted himself just reinforced me to get some of that, but use it differently. So, that type of skull agility is in my bones! That's why I was able to come up with the fruits of a good life."

Moments later, Mrs. Rodgers came back outside, and kissed her husband before she sat down, and hugged her daughter. Mrs. Rodgers stated, "I apologize for my behavior. I don't know what came over me. I just felt…huh, I just felt kind of…" Carlo looked at his beautiful wife and told her, "Baby, you don't have to explain. We just sitting outside having a family day. All that shit is behind us, and you know it. I haven't been in the life for years. Yes, I still kick it with a few of my partners, majority of them are dead now. I spend most of my time on the phone taking care of business, and making business trips. You already know that, and plus you have came along with me on those trips. So, chill on that shit!" Mrs. Rodgers just sat there quietly. Her facial expression was of confusing and embarrassment. She regretted her acts, she always displayed confidence and assurance of herself. For her daughter to see her act immature wasn't healthy for her daughter's emotional psychology as a woman. She shook it off, and told herself mentally, *that I'm glad I didn't act like this in front of my friends or out in public.* A few of us that are seasoned about mistakes, dig that mistakes are healthy and good, which aide in the process of becoming better and conscious of ourselves to be different to do better. Carlo "The Wiz" went on with his story, "Well while sitting there. Cat-Daddy told me that Mr. Sinclair and him owned the Lounge. I knew that was bullshit, since Black told me, he help run the spot. Cat Daddy stated, "Man, I took out a loan on my first Hog. See Mr. Sinclair, told me not to be a pimp, he said because the game isn't worth the time they are giving niggas. He instructed me on being a player in the game of life. Which is, if women was going to give me money, make sure that she already had some serious money, or she was ambitious enough to make something happen. But I still had to have my shit together. So, I took out that loan, and told him we can invest into the topless bar, and we did. Mr. Sinclair also owns a few restaurants in the Big Easy. That's where his wife is from. Her grandfather willed to her after her father passed, and between her sisters no one wanted to own the place, so she took it over, and the business has been doing good for the past fifteen or twenty years. On top of that I also own a barbershop and Laundromat. I'm thinking about jumping into some other shit. So pull my coat to how and when you going to make it in the big leagues greenie. The game you claiming to dive into without knowing the depth of that shit, is more serious than cancer." I just looked at this cocky-arrogant ass niggas, and replied, "Well get ready Mr. Cat-Daddy to get your feet wet in the game of big money, because that's exactly what I am going to do, you dig?" Cat-Daddy looked, and just cracked on my goal and delivery. That nigga didn't believe in nothing but himself, and Mr. Sinclair. I understood it as sure as dick and pussy works together for that great climax. Minutes later, while the Dj was setting up his equipment, and a few men in suits and ties, and young studs looking and dressed from the hip-hop area and culture fell in the place. They were dressed with their expensive jeans dropped low on their asses, wearing big gold cables around their necks, with gold watches, bracelets and rings. They were wearing so much gold it appears as though they were competing with King Tut. That were at the bar buying bottles of champagne, liquor and beer. It was fifteen guys in a pack talking loud and whooping and hollering. While Cat-Daddy was rolling up another gangster stick, and I was pouring myself another drink. I looked up and saw Black Jack hit the door, and then Mr. Sinclair was making his way up the few steps to where Cat-Daddy and I were sitting. Mr. Sinclair sat down and said, "So blood you are Stomp-Down's son huh?" I replied, "Yes Sir." Cat-Daddy dropped a lug on me, "I don't see how! The lil nigga too green." Mr. Sinclair commented, "Well that might be true, but we all started green in this game. Even I had to learn how to get hip to what was happening, and how to make shit happen in my favor. Even in the midst of so much bullshit, cut-throats, knavery, cunning, backstabbers, envy, hatred and pretenders. You have to be seasoned sooner or later being deep in this shit you will be. You see every player had to learn this game from a woman, and a season cat that got hip to game by a woman. How else can you learn how women are, if you ain't fucking with them to know what's really cracking. The woman needs a man's hardness and brains you dig? With that comes with protection, security and emotional connection. So, young-buck what's your plans.?" Cat-Daddy interjected, "He says he going big time on us hood niggas, ha…ha…ha." That Cat-Daddy nigga was really getting on my last fucking nerve, but I couldn't let him see me crack. Mr. Sinclair stated, "Young-buck I know you can be whatever you want to be, but there is one thing you need to remember about becoming a rich nigga, or anybody that's starting with nothing is this. In order to make it big, you either have to been born rich, very financially comfortable or you have to appear as though you are rich to get some serious bread. Which means that comes with game and intelligence to know what to do with the money in order to keep it. Once you get it, and keep it coming, then it's easier getting it, but harder to keep it." Mr. Sinclair was sitting like a king dress in a purple and white tailored made suit, with some purple and white gators. He was sharp as an razor-blade. He had on purple homburg on his aged dome of wisdom with small purple and white feather on the left side of his lid. Looking like a black king of some sort. Cat-Daddy shot some game at me, "When it comes to the species of women there are various types and some act like animals. I am not saying that women are animals. They are of a common origin that desire security, notoriety and love or some type of emotional content, but that various and is also very diversified among black women and white women according to their up bringing when they were little girls and teenagers, you dig? See the hood is like a big Amazon forest in this New World Order of getting it where and when you can. The game is infested with clichés, gangs and savage behavior called survival. People are acting like animals these days. You see animals attack each other for food and survival, but humans attack one another for money, material shit and to prove a point about who is the roughest and toughest nigga. Then, you have the sophisticated animals, which us the players and hustlers that play the game of life with finesse and style." Mr. Sinclair spoke sitting with his liquor in one hand and legs crossed. He spoke with a smooth slow tone mixed with great street philosophical savvy, " In this fucking concrete jungle, only a few remarkable cats rise above the mass of damn fools, by playing the game with a mystery aura of psychology power and will power. That's the shit that will take you far in life." Cat-Daddy commented, "In this fucking city, and all over the fucking world people are thirsty or hungry for all kinds of shit, and each want their taste of certain type of shit to feed their desires and wants from certain places and people, dig?" I thought to myself this nigga acts totally different around Mr. Sinclair he's more reserve and straight up, and not with all that mental shenanigans. I was soaking up game, like the earth soak up rain, you dig? Mr. Sinclair went on with game, "There are many things you need to know, but remember this, women are going to try you. They want to see if you mean want you say, are you serious or a joker, do you know what you want, and what are you willing to do to make that happen. Basically, do you have a plan. Don't get to locked on the woman's sex. I don't care if that woman has the best pussy you ever had in your life. Then, she feel as though she can keep you in check with her pussy. Once the woman thinks that her pussy got you hooked, then she becomes your kryptonite, then you can never be her hero or Black Superman. Whenever she offers it, turn it down. When she has done something that's grand for you. Give her some dick! Make sure it's something that will be a tool or something worthy for her to give to you. When she gives you something like sex, now she thinks she has to keep giving you this, to keep you in her control mode. Put limits and parameters on that sexual tool. Sex can be a hypnotic tool. Now, when you put that dick on her with some psychological game, with some value of goals setting. She's convinced she can't waste your time, because what you have achieved speaks for its self, you dig?" Melody asked her father, "What was going through your mind at that time. Was it too much to take in or what?" Carlo replied, "Well baby-girl, I mean some of this game my father would just give me the tip of the iceberg, because he thought I was too young at the time. Later when he stopped, or couldn't work any more. We talked about this a little more when I was in the 12th grade, and before he died. Some of it I was familiar with." Melody put her father on the spot with her next question, "Did you use any of that stuff on mom?" Carlo "The Wiz" bellowed, "What! Some I used to keep her, because I knew she was going to be my wife. All the low-down hood stuff, no. The psychological aspiration and inspiration yes! Your mother was a teacher, so I had to be intelligent of some sort. I had to have goals, dreams and a purpose. If I didn't have any of those qualities and value we wouldn't be your parents."

Moments later school kids were getting off the bus, and walking home in all different directions. Carlo got up to check the pit to ensure the fire and smoke was going out slowly as usual. He could hear his wife and daughter talking low amongst themselves, but he really couldn't make it out what they were really talking about. He told himself it was concerning the question his daughter asked. *He knew he handled it cleverly and clean.* Then he walked back to join his family. There were times throughout his marriage he had to catch himself from going player on his wife, but he also knew he couldn't get all of that street venom out of his veins. He knew biologically his father injected that venom from his seminal fluid, which was the makeup of his DNA. Plus, mentally he phantom that his mother was a strong lady to endure that power from his father, and for him to be here. When the right woman and man come together can't nothing but death separate them. But how many of us find that right partner to overcome life's challenges with loyalty to one another?

A Cold Summer

The sun was starting to set, and Carlo "The Wiz" Rodgers and his family were still in the backyard chilling. Carlo "The Wiz" kept right on with his story of how he became a rich nigga. Carlo "The Wiz" continued, "Well, I will try to make this story short as possible, so baby-girl won't get home too late." Melody replied, "Daddy I'll just spend the night here." Mrs. Rodgers interjected with fury, "Like hell you will! You are going to take your ass home. See that's the problem with relationships and marriages with you young people. You young folk don't look at the whole picture and see the effect of things ya'll do or doing. Then, ya'll will turn around and point the finger for receiving ya'll wrong actions." Melody asked, "What's wrong with staying over at my parents. The home I was born and raised in. What's wrong with that?" Mrs. Rodgers stated, "Baby-girl do you know the message you would send to your husband the moment you don't come home. Even if you spend one night here with your parents. See, baby-girl men's' minds doesn't work like ours. They see things from a different point and perspective than we do. A good wholesome relationship or marriage has to have respect, dignity, honor, loyalty before it becomes true undying love. True love! Once your husband's mind begins to think those type of things like why you had to stay over at your parents, what's wrong and he will feel like you are not telling him the truth, and you know that you are telling the truth. That's when the shit hits the fan. Excuse my French, baby." Melody replied, "But Ralph isn't like that!" Mrs. Rogers responded, "Honey, you want to explain to Miss Greenie here?" Carlo "The Wiz" stated smoothly and serene, "Baby-girl look, what your mother is trying to tell you is that majority of men today isn't like your father, Hah, ha…" Sunshine Rogers commented, "Come on honey quit playing and tell her what's wrong about that shit before she messes off a good man." Carlo took his daughter's hands and looked into her beautiful innocent brown eyes, and stated, "Baby-girl listen, men today are very insecure creatures. I'm not saying that my son-in-law is insecure, but you both come from different times and had different experiences that your mother and I experienced. Those experiences made us what we are today and our future. The way we raised you, is the lady we want you to become, and you have. Never miss one night staying or laying in the same bed with your husband, never! If one of us whether it's me or your mother were to ever get sick, only then will you be obligated to staying many days and nights. Once a man gets into his head, or have an inkling of a doubt that you might be seeing another man. The trust and love will slowly fade away. Same if you was thinking or have inkling of a doubt about your husband seeing another woman, you wouldn't want to be in that relationship. Am I right?" Melody looked at her father's sincerity, and a tear rolled down her cheek. She hugged here father tightly and stated, "I love you daddy you are great father. I understand now." Her father responded that he loved her also. Melody leaned over and hugged her mother stating she was the greatest mother in the whole world. Then Melody asked, "So mother you never spend one night away from dad?" Her mother said, "Only when my mother was sickly, and your father would come to hospital every night and stay for hours, and pop right back up early that morning. My mother told me one night before she passed away. Lying there in that hospital bed." Mrs. Rogers was choking up as she was telling her daughter, what her mother told her. "Momma was still a beauty with that soft beige complexion skin, and her salt and pepper silky and shiny hair. She was weak, pale and gasping for air, but she was determined to tell me something. I kept telling her to rest. She just would not let it go. So, I asked mother with tears in my eyes, and tears started rolling down her beautiful ruddy cheek. What is it mom? What is it? She said with all determination to speak, 'Sunshine that's a good man. Don't you do anything stupid to run him off. I can see love in that man's eyes and in his demeanor that he really loves and care about you. It reminds me of the way your father looked. I was is most treasured prize and concern. Don't never let your friends,or outsiders dictate your emotions and feelings that you have for that man. You know you love him very much. If you love him, huh…love him, and if you don't huh… let him go.' Mrs. Rodgers was having trouble telling this story to her daughter. Even when she told her husband years ago it was complicated, and still remains hard to tell. Then mom said, 'Because the only thing you will have is problems and pretensions, huh… which brings a trouble mind and a heavy heart.' That's when I knew that your father was the man for me. He did some things I didn't like or didn't understand some of those things. When mother spoke highly of him, I started looking at the things that he was doing a little different. Basically, I was trying to see things from my mother's point of view. I wish your grandfather could have met your father. I know he would have said the same thing. Baby sometimes the coldest truth, gives the greatest warmth." Melody was soaking up everything her parents were informing her about life. How life can be cold but yet warmly beautiful when you know your place, and see the wonder of real grace.

Gettin' Hip To Stackin' Chips

As the sun started making its way westward to set within several hours. The family moved from the backyard on to the front of the house, and sat on the large porch. The porch had several chairs, and also a solid wooden swing. Carlo "The Wiz" leaped from his seat, and went to retrieved the large fan that was left in the backyard, and brought it back to the garage. It was a four car garage with three expensive vehicles, and a basic pickup truck. Carlo only drove the truck, when materials were needed. Being a property owner or landlord came with responsibilities, and duties whenever his tenants had home issues of some sort to be repaired. Carlo went inside the house, and retrieved three bottles of water. Before he took his seat, that was on the front porch, he gave his wife and daughter each a bottle of water, and opened his while taking a seat. At this point Carlo "The Wiz" said, "Well let me continue to reveal how the rich get richer, the poor stay poor and how I got rich. I had to put some serious things in motion, you dig? Rich people will take a risk to get rich, and chances for more advances for a certain lifestyle.

That's when I started making moves from the streets to the millionaire seats. I was twenty-two at the time. I started hanging out at the Foxx Inn Lounge a little more. One night while talking with this young chic. Her name was Merci Beauty Batiste, but her stage name was "Juicy." I will never forget that name." His wife asked, "Why?" Carlo responded, "Because I never heard a name like that before in my life. It's a very different name." His wife interjected again, "The name Juicy or Merci?" Carlo "The Wiz," "Well, Merci Beauty of course! There's nothing different about the word juicy. Anyway, while I was sitting there plotting my moves, and I needed a female at this point in the game. Plus, I needed more money. I was getting like $ 700 a month from one of my properties I was renting out at the time. While chilling Merci caught my attention. She was at the bar with her other female co-workers having a drink. I said to myself internally, *that's the one right there*. She will be the partner I needed. She's young, beautiful and very appealing. But I had to find out her age, and where her mind was at. I knew she had to be of age to be working or dancing in this joint. Before the club starting jumping, a few more of the girls or ladies came from the back and had a few drinks, with the other women that was already at the bar. They were wearing their sexy erotic outfits for the customers to throw money, and drink and keep spending that money. The name of the game is have a good time, and throw plenty of dimes. When Merci looked over at me, I signaled for her to come over. She was walking toward me, and she looked like the reincarnation of Cleopatra. With walnut looking skin, and beautiful shaped breast, hips that stuck out like side view mirrors, and coal black shiny hair that bounced as she walked. I was dressed in a pressed white shirt with blue round cufflinks that matched my blue vest and blue eel skin shoes. I didn't wear a tie. I never really liked wearing ties. So, I stood up when she approached the table. We introduced ourselves, then I proceeded to put my game into effect. Once I found out that she was going to nursing school, and dancing to pay her tuition fees, classes and books. I asked where she was living? She said, "I am living with my sister. That have five kids, working at a burger joint making $7. 50 hour, in a one bedroom apartment, and I couldn't let her struggle with all those kids by herself." I commented, "Where's the father?" Merci replied, "Two kids have the same father, but the other three have different fathers. My father kicked her out when she had the first two. She's always working over time, and she rarely gets to see her kids. So, I started working there too, but it wasn't enough money trying to help her and go to school at the same time. I was still living with my parents, but when they found out I was dancing they kicked me out also, and that's when I moved in with her. Then we move into a two bedroom apartment. I've been living with my sister, and going to school and dancing. I just can't wait to finish! That way, I can get on with my career and make some real money, without this bullshit hassle in this business." I saw an open door, and I stepped right into it. I said, "Look here, I have a plan that can help both of us achieve our goals, if you not afraid." Merci asked, "What's the plan?" Before I started to unravel my game plan I was rudely interrupted by "Cat Daddy." He bellowed, "Bitch don't you have work to do?" She slid from her seat, and looked disappointed. I told her, "We'll finish later or some other time." Cat Daddy sat down in the seat across from me looking coldly into my eyes, and spoke with a cold tight whisper, "Look nigga, I don't know what you trying to pull, but the bitches, the ladies or felines are off limits, except for the customers. If you are a customer only then can you have a long customer and worker conversation with anyone of them. Until then it's about getting a lap dance. Little nigga respect the business, and stay the fuck away from that jazzy little thing that was sitting here with you. She's a real money maker in here. You get my drift?" I just sat there looking right into that nigga's eyes, and didn't say a word. He asked coldly, "Lil' nigga did you hear what I said?" I still didn't say a word I was psychologically psyching him out ." Melody asked, "Why?" Her father replied, "That's when you get deep within another person's psychology, and start taking over their psychology with their own mind and thoughts. Which means they will start some internal angling to figure you out even more when you don't respond verbally. Because when you speak you give people an edge on how you feel, what you are thinking and what your intentions are. I wasn't going to give that nigga that. I was making him look like the sucka and hater he really was. See most people get fooled, misused and abused by being too naïve or afraid, so they loose the game before they began. I had to stick to my script. I had come to far to turn back, and if I did turn back I would found myself back in the same situation that killed my father. Which was working hard with little or nothing to show for it. I got up from my seat while all the while looking at this hating ass nigga that I thought was cool, and down ass dude. Over the years the more I talked with this nigga the more I saw this nigga had a deep down hatred for niggas that was doing good for themselves. That's one of the major problems we have as black people until this very day. When our ancestors has shown by the written history, that building anything massive is a collective coterie, and the shit that our ancestors created has filled museums around the world. The pillagers has made and are making billions and millions of dollars from our ancestors creation. Collective work for the greater good of the whole is better, rather than a few for the few. Unfortunately, that's the way it has always been. Major work, but a few are willing to do the job. I stood up and stated, "You finish?" Cat Daddy responded, "Yeah lil nigga. Don't make me repeat myself, you get my drift?" I had to get under this nigga's collar, when I noticed that a few people in the place were looking at us. I shot back, "I got yours, now get mine! Stay out my way and my business ole' hating wanna be ass player. Polish up your game, before you fall with them lames. Later chump!" I walked by him nonchalantly, he just turned and watched me hit the door. I thought the nigga was going to do something stupid. I did wanted him to make a stupid or silly play. He just cracked a crooked grin. As I walked by."

"My money from over the four years of saving grew enough for me to start making these moves. That's a major problem for blacks to save in order to invest, and become a millionaire or financially comfortable if they choose too. But many of our people just consume, consume and never obtain anything that's worthy for the next generation." Carlo "The Wiz" was determined not to be one of those lazy, no goal setting ass nigga and trying to get something for nothing ass nigga. To him that's a loser's mentality.

"I stayed away from the Lounge for about a week. I was sitting on the couch in the living-room flipping through the yellow pages looking for a good lawyer. I wanted an attorney that has been practicing law for more than ten to fifteen years. I heard a knock on the door. I got up and peeped through the peep hole of the door, it was Merci. I opened the door with much enthusiasm, and welcoming her in. I told her to make herself comfortable, and would she like anything to drink or eat. She just wanted some water, so I went into the kitchen to get her a bottle. Then, I asked how did you get my address?" She replied, "I asked Black Jack, since I haven't seen much of you at the club. I mean at the lounge since that episode with "Cat Daddy." I shot back, " I knew that nigga was a hater from our first conversation years ago. Anyway, what brings you by?" Carlo "The Wiz" knew what brought her by, he was just playing his hand and psychological cards for her to reveal her intentions, thoughts and feelings. Which is always the hook. Because the spoken word is powerful to the subconscious mind, which make things move forward from that unseen to the concrete manifestation. Most people do not understand the power of words, and what it does to the human mind. "Merci responded, "Our last and first conversation was about, if I remember correctly, was about helping each other." Carlo lend back on the sofa, and popped his feet up on the coffee table. While Merci was sitting in one of the plush chairs with her legs crossed revealing her well shaped legs, all the way up to her helium shapely thighs, due to her mini skirt she was wearing. Carlo "The Wiz" shot back, "Well, you said you were tired of the bullshit that was going on at the Lounge. What I am putting down is going to pay off heavily, but it's going to demand of you to play this game tight. I mean airtight, you dig?" Merci looked at him with those seductive eyes of hers, and her heart was beating fast, her nipples became hard, and pussy was getting moist by the minute. To her Carlo was a very handsome, smart, clever, very masculine and mysterious man. She only been with one other guy in her life that was when she was in high school. Her boyfriend slept with her best friend, and she really wasn't into guys for years. She was focused on her studies, and very determine to finish. She felt deep within her being that Carlo was the man she has been looking for all her life. A man with a plan, discipline, intelligent and could handle himself. Merci asked, " So, what is it that I have to do?" I told her, "You going to be my personal secretary. I already have the room set up with a desk, a phone, and some index cards you will have to read off, whenever a certain person calls. There's a card for every type of clientele that calls." Carlo told Merci to follow him into the other room which was right off from the living quarter where they were sitting. The room that his mother had turn into a den, but he turned into a home office with a computer, a laptop, printers, company machine, a shredder, box full of blank index cards, a rolodex of the businesses and people that he was already connected to, due to his real estate or two homes that he rented out. Carlo had to hustle and bustle to cop that second home. But shit still wasn't totally in his favor financially. The desk faced the window to see who was coming while the blinds were practically open. Next, she followed him to one of the bedrooms. The home had three bedrooms. She looked at him hesitantly, she was horny and wet for him. She thought he was making a sexual pass at her. She was thinking to herself, *damn he sure is moving fast. I would love to make love to him, but not that fast.* Carlo read her face and stated, "No, it's nothing like that. This is your bedroom." Merci asked, "You want me to live here with you? No! No, I can't do that to my sister. She needs my help." Carlo "The Wiz" stated, " This plan is going to help everybody! You, your sister, those kids and me." Merci looked at him, and thought *how was this nigga really going to put it down for all us.* She was more intrigued and interested to knowing how this plan was going to work for everyone. She was amazed when they were standing in the office room. There was a wall filled with books, and other reading materials. Here she was going to college for a career, so reading was a must. But here is this man not going to nobody's college or university, and he had a library full of books. That was the icing on the cake for her to go ahead with Carlo "The Wiz's plan.

Mrs. Rogers got up from her seat and went into the house, and grabbed the other small can of superb-herb for her husband. Then, she went to use the restroom. She was having an emotional battle concerning what she was hearing from here husband. She knew he left some of the story out when he first told her on how he became a rich man. She smiled to herself, and became aware that he was telling their daughter everything, and told her what he thought she needed to know, and how she can contain it. She smiled and shook her head while sitting on the toilet, and whispered to herself with great admiration for her husband, 'that's Wiz.' She wiped herself, then rose from the toilet. She flushed it, and washed her hands, then headed back to the front porch to hear the story unfold. Melody was coming from the other restroom, when her mother and her ran into each other while headed back to the front porch. They both sat back down to join Carlo. Melody said, "We're back now." Carlo "The Wiz" went on with his story, " The next day after telling Merci what I needed for her to do. I caught the city bus down to the rental car service. I called in advance, and told them to hold a black Jag for me. I needed a car that was not cheap, but also not too expensive." Melody asked, "Why?" Mrs. Rogers stated, "I was just going to ask the same thing." Carlo "The Wiz" cracked, "If I'm seen in a car that was already high priced, that means when I grow, I would have to a buy a very expensive car for my progress to be seen. And that would cost me more money, before I have made the money. So, if I start with a Mercedes, that means I have to get another high priced ride like a Rolls Royce or some type of classic high price car. My goal was to get rich and stay rich, and not getting caught up into all that material shit. It's easy if you are not cognitive of it, which is useless spending. When you spend money, what you are really doing is throwing away a valuable resource. That's another reason why majority of blacks are poor and struggling financially, because they purchase shit they don't need. They buy shit for silly and useless reasons. I went down to the rental car place. I was dressed in my business attire, and paid the fee, and took out the address for the lawyers office. When I arrived at the Tower Inn Building. I took three deep breathes, and said to myself and the universe, *Lets' get rich, and play this game from the streets to the millionaire seats.* I entered the building and looked at the platform that displayed suite numbers, floors and names. The name of the lawyer was exactly what and who I was looking for. Abram Bernstein. I had my briefcase, and jumped on the elevator to the ninth floor. I walked down this long hallway when I got off the elevator. I entered suite 906, and there was a reddish-brunette female sitting at the front desk. She looked slightly old, with gray eyes, wrinkled hands with several rings on her fingers. Her voice was very raspy, which indicated she probably was a heavy smoker. Her hair was upon her head like camel's hump. Then she asked, "How can I help you?" I replied, "I am here to see Mr. Bernstein. I have a 10 a.m. appointment." She responded, "Have a seat, and I will inform him that you are here." About fifteen or twenty minutes went by, and she stated, "You can go in now." "I told her thank you, and went in. This guy was wearing some thick glasses, he was partially bald, he stood about six feet tall, and was very slender. He was wearing a very expensive suit. We shook hands, and introduced ourselves. When we both sat down, I couldn't help but noticed he was wearing a gold Rolex watch also. Ole' Bernstein asked, "What can I do for you?" I responded, " I need to retain a good lawyer." Mr. Bernstein asked, " Are you in some type of trouble of some sort." I replied, "No. I just need a damn good lawyer with experience, and that's very influential." Bernstein lend back in his chair from the other side of the desk, and ask another question, "What kind of influence are you looking for?" I replied, "Great economical influence. That kind that helped you reached your goal as being a very successful lawyer." Bernstein asked numerous of questions. I must admit I was prepared for the questions he needed to ask. So I replied, "I studied your practice, it's all public record nothing is hidden, plus I don't think a broke or financial person would be wearing a $30,000 watch, if he couldn't retain the image." Bernstein replied, " You are very observant. I must admit, I do know some very rich and powerful people. But they might be a little out of your league. These are some very global or international people. Very sophisticated people!" I had to hit him like this for an angle, and for that door to open. Melody asked, "What door and what did you hit him with. In order for him to open the door you needed open?" Carlo "The Wiz" went on, "The door of opportunity, and Baby-girl I had to use that race card. The race card is economical, not skin color bullshit. So, I asked him, "You mean they don't do business with young black men, or what you are telling me, is that I am too broke, and don't have enough money or I'm not intelligent enough to enter that elite rich circle.?" Bernstein face turned slightly red, and he spoke, "Why do your people do that! They always think everything and everybody is a racist or black and white racial issues! Okay, you want to get into that inner circle. Basically, what you are looking for is a rich mentor, right. Am I right." I told him. "No! I want to get into that inner circle to invest money, and I need a good lawyer like yourself to respresent my economical interest like you have did concerning your other rich clients." Bernstein just smiled, and lend back in his chair again. Then he asked, "What school or college you went to?" Carlo "The Wiz" went on, "Baby-girl I knew I had him then. Now, he has to prove to me that he wasn't prejudice. He knew that I was clever that's why he asked what school I went to. Anyway, I threw $5000 in cash on the desk. He looked at it, and put it into his inner suit pocket, and retrieve some papers for me to sign. I told him that I will take the papers with me, and read over them tonight, and bring them back tomorrow." He said, "That's fine! And that's smart." We shook hands, then he stated, "I'll walk you out, plus I need to get something from the car." I knew he was trying to get a better angle on me, and mainly to see what I was driving. The car would indicate whether I was bluffing about having money. We jumped on the elevator, and moments later arrived on the fifth floor, and walked into the parking garage, making small talk. Then he asked, "What floor are you parked on?" I told him the 5th floor. He replied I'm on the 9th floor. I have a reserved parking spot." He asked what kind of car I drove? I told him, "A Jaguar, but I was thinking about getting rid of it." Bernstein asked, "What's wrong with it, those are some pretty good cars. That was my wife's first car when my practice started taking off, now she has a Mercedes SUV and I have a Mercedes S500." I replied, " When my business grow some more, maybe I get myself one, plus that's what I contemplating." Bernstein, "Oh, that reminds me, you never stated what type of business you were in." I reached in my vest pocket next to my pocket watch with chains hanging, and gave him one of my business cards. He read it, "Real Estate. That reminds me, here's one of my cards, better yet here's a few more in case you want to give some to other people you might know or that could use my service." I told him, "Thank you, but first before I pass these cards to other businesses and trusted people that I know. I must see how you handle your new client's business first, until then I will set them on my desk at the office." We shook hands again and departed.

"When I was driving, and headed back home, my cell phone was ringing, it was Merci on the other line. I answered she spoke, " Hey, I just received a phone call from a Bernstein Law Firm. They were calling to see were here at the office, but I read the index card that you were out of the office today. It was some lady on the line. She sounded old, and she said she will try contacting you on tomorrow. And also, I have some disappointing news. One of your family renters were moving out. They just call to give there 30-day notice." I told her, "Thank you I'm on the way back. When I hung up the phone, I became little angry. Right when everything seems to be working out, I got hit with this shit. That means my money was taking a dive, and drastically if I didn't get another family or renter into that home. I screamed damn, and damn ran into the back of a car in front of me."

"When I got home, and pulled in the driveway. Merci came out like she was my wife of some sort. I never looked at her as my girlfriend or companion. I saw her as my business partner. She looked at me with a sense of concern." She asked, " How did it go today, other than the news about one of renters moving out?" Melody ask, "Do you think she was very concerned about how you were feeling?" Her father answered, "I was going to figure that out. So, I can know where she was at mentally, emotionally, and economically. I had to control myself. I didn't want go off on her, if I did she would have the wrong impression of me, and break out. Right at this piont I needed her. I had to be out in the field, or moving around. While someone was at the office making and receiving phone calls. I had to keep up my business image, and persona by all means. She followed me into the home office, and I sat behind the desk. She sat in one of the chairs that were in front of the desk. I told her, "That Bernstein Firm is a law firm I went to earlier. I knew he was going to call. That was his secretary that called, and I know he told her to make the call to see if I was on the up and up." Merci replied, "It was a woman, but had a very real deep raspy voice." I was spinning the black plush desk chair back and forth thinking and contemplating my next move. I was thinking so deeply I forgot that Merci and I was conversing. Then I spoke, "That's cool. Was there any other calls." I was sitting there making and designing my moves, but I had to get her to think and believe shit was deeper than they actually were." Mrs. Rodgers asked, "Why were you lying to her instead of telling her the truth. It could have back fired on you." Melody stated, "Yes dad, I was about to say the same thing." Carlo "The Wiz" grinning, and his wife always called that grin the devil's grin. Then he stated, "I knew that was a chance I was taking. I had to make that move, because I was going into over-drive. I didn't want to be thought of or seen as a liar. Then, Merci would be out the picture. Plus, I had the rental car for three days. I had to make my move inside the business world while I had the car, which was seen or appeared that I had some kind of money." Merci stated with excitement while in the office, "Why don't you purchase or look into purchasing some foreclosed homes?" I looked at her and commented, "That's a good idea, but right now that's not a good move. Because the money to purchase, and hold the home is a little tight." Merci replied, "Go to the bank, and get a loan where you bank at!" I smiled and told her, "Damn, that's why I wanted you on this project. I need somebody smart around me!" Mrs. Rodgers asked, "So did you go to the bank?" Her husband cracked, "No I didn't. I went to see Mr. Sinclair the week before, when I wasn't going to the Lounge. I hooked up with Black Jack, and spoke to him about my next move. And I talked with Mr. Sinclair several times about my goals. One time "Cat Daddy" was there trying to knock me in front of Mr. Sinclair. So, he already knew what I was trying to accomplish. Plus, going to him was a way of not having to pay interest on the borrowed money. He told me that he would support me anytime I needed his help. And he loved and admire me for not fucking with junk or exploiting our women. I was to pay him back whenever I get the whole thing. I wanted to see how Merci think. I wanted to make sure that I had another mind around with ideas. That way I would be able to keep myself in check, and plus I had to make a step above everyone that I came across. I jumped up and out of the chair, and ran over and kissed her on the cheek. I told her, "Hell yes! Damn you smart!" Merci replied, "Actually while I was sitting here studying for one of my semester examines. I started reading through one those books about real estate investing, and the idea just popped in my head when you said that. I know know that, you probably just forgot from all the activites that's going on. It's possible it might have slipped your mind." I went into the kitchen, instead cutting through the living quarters. I went down the hallway. She yelled, "Oh, there is some fried chicken, mashed potatoes and green beans on the stove!" I heard her voice getting clearer as she was approaching the kitcken. I was fixing myself a plate, I stated, "Thank you! You didn't have to do this. We are business partners." Merci replied, "I know that! But since you aren't charging me anything for living here. I thought that's the least I can do for you. Now, I can help my sister more, and now she doesn't have to work all that overtime. She's able to spend some quality time with her kids, thanks to you. I still dance some nights, and work in the office during the day." I threw up my hands and asked her, "What about your classes?" Merci spoke, "I do online classes, since I'm living here. My nephew broke my laptop, and I really didn't have the money at the time to get a new one. You have one here, and I knew you wouldn't mind, if I used this one." I replied back, "Oh, okay. I don't want you to play around or get too complacent about your schooling. That's your ticket for success, and it's part of my responsibility to ensure you achieve that." Merci grabbed my hand and stated, "I know, and it just reinforces what you said about this plan of yours would help everyone, and it is. I see it clearly." Merci was talking seductively. Carlo had to catch himself, but his wife helped him with that endeavor. Mrs. Rodgers blurted, "Oh, she was getting romantic with you huh?" Carlo said, "She was, but I didn't buy into that shit. I knew I had to keep encouraging her to handle my shit, until my business and money was much bigger. The $5000 that I gave to the lawyer was from the $10,000 that I had saved over the years from my two rental properties. I did asked Mr. Sinclair for the money, because he owned a restaurant and few rental properties himself, and not forgetting the Foxx Inn Lounge. He wasn't a millionaire, but he was financially comfortable. He digs what it takes for a young nigga to make money moves coming from the bottom, other than selling drugs and pimping women. I was angry at Mr. Sinclair at the time, because I didn't understand what I understood now. Melody asked, "What was it you didn't understand?" Carlo lend forward and looked his daughter straight in the eyes, and held her hand and spoke, "Mr. Sinclair told me that if he gave me that $10,000 he wasn't helping me. He would actually be hurting me", Carlo said. His daughter Melody chimed serenely, "How would that be hurting someone that's trying to make a difference in their life." Carlo replied still holding his daughter's hand, "If he would have given me that money, he would have taken away my creative juices to create, and come up with needed answers. Which is to shape and mold me through all my tears, ambition, sweat and frustrations. Without all those human elements playing their part on becoming successful, I would have taken my success for granted. I wouldn't have valued my success, the money and the lifestyle. I probably would have lost it at all, and the major question would be, what was all that for? Now, I understand. If you don't strive for it, hustle for it, lose sleep for it and willing to die for it, then you don't want it. And I thank him for refusing to give me that money. It has made me a strong, smart, disciplined and a thankful person. The wisdom and the discipline is in the process. The person you become is a better you, through that struggle for success. So now you, your mother and your son can enjoy the good life. And believe me Baby-girl it was all worth it! And another thing I will make mention why we are on the subject. That's one of the main reasons majority of the people never become successful, especially our people. They feel as though somebody owe them something, and they want to have a million dollars. That's stupid to want something that's bigger than your mind can conceive, and plus, they can't handle having $500 to $1000. If you don't know what to do with $500 or $1000, you can forget about being a millionaire. Some people have became millionaires with less money. It's like asking for a blessing, and not knowing what a blessing is." Melody and her mother looked at each other and smiled. Melody said, "Dad did Merci, the chic that was living with you at the time. Did shhee... every try to make a move on you?" Carlo thought to himself about that question. Internally he thought *was his daughter trying to be messy, or was she that naïve to ask a question like that.* Carlo "The Wiz" pulled some of that slick shit out of his bag. Then he spoke, "You know baby-girl she did, and I had to remind her this was all business, and no personal or pleasure was involved." Carlo stuck to the script, which is some shit should never be told or unfolded. There's an old saying that says, 'there is a lot of untold shit in the graves, if you go there at night you will the hear some of the deepest shit that's only for the brave.'

When Carlo's wife came out of the house with his superb-herb, he thanked her for bringing it. As he was rolling himself a gangster stick. He continued on with his story from the streets to millionaire seats. " I got up from eating and talking with Merci, and went back to the office, and called Mr. Sinclair. His wife answered the phone, and then he spoke, "Hello." I replied, "Hey Unk, it's your nephew "Lil' Stomp." Before Carlo could say anything he was cut off by his daughter, "Why did you call him? Did you ask again to borrow money?" Carlo popped, "No, I needed his lawyer to look over the documents that I got from my lawyer. I wanted someone that wasn't part of the interest or endavour to see the flaw or bogus contract, if it was one. Mr. Sinclair told me that he would call me back after he got in contact with his lawyer. About thirty-minutes later, the phone ranged. It was Mr. Sinclair telling me the lawyer said fax it over, or bring it by his home about an hour later. I started reading while waiting for an hour to make my next move. The phone ranged again, this time it was Mr. Bernstein, "May I speak with Mr. Rodgers?" I replied, "This is Mr. Rodgers speaking. How can I help you?" Mr. Bernstein said, "Are you still coming by tomorrow?" I started thinking either this guy is setting me up for something or he thinks I'm bluffing." So to keep him in the dark, and wanting to get an angle or feel for me I had to make him see his vulnerability. So I replied, "Excuse me Mr. Bernstein, but I need to take this long distance call. This an overseas call." Then I just hung up the phone. The phone ranged again, but I didn't answer it. I yelled at Merci, "I'm leaving!" I didn't hear her respond back. I walked to her room, and she was lying their in bed sleeping. I slightly closed the door, and headed to Prosperity Street, where Mr. Sinclair lived. The homes in this area was worth $500,000 and up. I pulled up to this gate after pushing in the home number. Mr. Sinclair's voice was blasting through the gate speaker, "Who is it!" I replied, "Your nephew!" The gate slowly opened, and I drove on up through the large black steel gate with a large brick stone columns on both sides. Mr. Sinclair's home was massive compaired to this one I'm living in now. I pulled up in the Large C shaped driveway. There was a large sculptured stone lion inside the waterfall fountain. The water was coming out of the stone lion's mouth. The yard was greatly manicured. I was thinking, I didn't think Mr. Sinclair was living this large. I knew he wore expensive suits, shoes, watches and drove expensive cars. But he was so low key, and I would have never thought this. I thought for a second, how does he live like this, with a just a few businesses. I ranged the doorbell, and this young lady came to the door. It wasn't his wife. I introduced myself. Moments later Mr. and Mrs. Sinclair came from a long hallway. We all embraced each other. He introduced me to his grand-daughter. She was several years older than me. She was a nice looking woman for her age. As we were standing at the door embracing, and making small talk. The doorbell ranged. Mr. Sinclair opened it, and this tall cocoa looking brother come in. His name was

Nicholas "Bulldog" Williams. He must slip through the slow smooth closing gates, after I entered. Mr. Sinclair led Mr. Williams and myself to his large office. Mr. Sinclair spoke, "Bulldog this is my nephew Mr. Rodgers. He has a contract that he would like for you to look over before he signs it." Mr. Bulldog spoke with a high pitched voice, "That's smart of you young man. Not many of our people read fine print, or know how to read contracts, they just sign with a naïve notion to trust so easy." I replied, "Thank you sir." Mr. Sinclair and myself just sat there quietly. After Mr. Sinclair's attorney finished flipping through the pages, then he spoke, "It's legit." Mr. Williams, asked, "Young man you don't mind me asking?" I told him, "No sir, I don't mind if you ask your question." He asked, "Why are you going in business with a Jew." I told him, "Who other than Jews have great respect for money, business, has a great desire to be a merchant of some sort and also have great economical and political connections?" Mr. Bulldog Williams stated, "I must admit you are right about that. But there are some very powerful and rich blacks also." I commented, "I know there are, but I only know one personally, and we are sitting in his home right now. And he trusts my judgement on what I'm doing in order for me to become rich and powerful." Mr. "Bulldog" Williams rose from his chair. And shook Mr. Sinclair hand, and shook my hand also. I reached into my pocket to pay for his service. The he told me, "That wont be necessary. If you ever need my service or if there is anything I can do to help you just let me know. Here is my card. Ya'll men have a good day." Then, he made an exit from the room."

Mr. Sinclair and Carlo "The Wiz" stepped outside in the backyard. The landscaped backyard was beautifully constructed. There was a grill and BBQ pit, greeny lawn that was huge. The were several huge stone boulders that were stacked in a constructive design, and the midst of the well desidned stones was a Jacuzzi. Inside one of the stone near the Jacuzzi was a 50" flat screen TV. They sat down in some of the chairs that encircled a large table with the large umbrella in the certain. Carlo went on revealing the ways and means that he became a rich nigga that came from the bottom, which was the hood. Looking at all this rich living from a just a few years ago when I met Mr. Sinclair and I didn't know he lived like this. Here it was four or more years later, that this man that he admired was willing to show him where, and how he lived. Carlo "The Wiz" spoke, "Baby-girl I was a little warm under the collar about being there with this man that I admired. I thought I knew this guy. He knew my father, and Black Jack also, but them niggas never invited cats to their homes. I had to compose myself. I couldn't hold it much longer. I knew he had to have a legit reason, because my father didn't have friends come to the house when I was coming up neither. So, I asked Mr. Sinclair, how are you able to live like this, with the few businesses you have. This has to be a million dollar home. He replied, "No it's half of million dollar home. I'm put you down with some game about wanting to live good and getting there. Especially where we come from. I want you to never forget what I'm about to tell you nephew. I like it that you started calling me uncle. That let's me know that you have a certain type of respect for yourself, and the ones that's older and helpful. Mainly, because of your father. Your father was a man's man, in every way. The way youngsters are being raise is silly and irresponsible. But that comes from their parents. See you always hear these young parents say I'm give my kids what I didn't have, and what do they give them, material shit! Without resources of mind and discipline to go with it. I think you are beginning to see this yourself. No man can achieve or gain any type of real money without some type of discipline with money. How can millions of dollar come to anybody that can't handle having one-hundred dollars. If you knew that I couldn't handle that volume of money that I work hard for, and ask you to borrow some money, would you give me some money? Especially, if I stay broke. You or nobody is going to keep giving me some money, if I don't know how to keep some, you dig?" Mrs. Rodgers commented, "That makes a lot of sense!" Her husband replied, " Yes, it does. To give anyone that keeps repeating the same shit, and I keep aiding and aiding them. All I'm doing is handicapping them to remain weak, and never change their bad habits. And at the same time I'm losing money, because after a while they won't be able to pay you back. One failure leads to another failure, which is irresponsibility. Then I asked Mr. Sinclair, "Why you waited four years to invite me to your home?" Mr. Sinclair, "Nephew, you youngsters trust to easily. And that's because today many of the youngsters grow up with ya'll mothers, and live their too long. Then unconsciously you began picking up the women traits of trust and friendliness with meek and mild ways about life. I know you came up different, because of your father. But I had to wait until you were serious about the life you choose. If you were to go back on what you said you were going to do, how can I trust you, if you can't trust yourself or stick to your words. If you didn't stick to your own words, then why should I. Those are your words, so if your words don't mean a damn thing to you, why should they mean a damn to me. Since, you stuck to your words for years. Hustling and trying to make something happen for you, I respect that! It wasn't easy for me either. It's not easy for any of us niggas coming from the hood to make good, to trust. One thing about the hood that I will always love, is the hood made me a hustler, a predator and a nigga with game. See, once you get a taste of having money, you will do anything to fufill your desire to have that and some more. But majority of us in the hood never get a chance to have real money in our hands. Then, we see the hustlers, the pimps, the players and other down ass niggas out there getting money. So we see that, and then we want it. So, pimping, selling drugs and that other shit that leads to envy, jeaoulsy and all that leads to black on black crime. And today they call that being true to the hood. How can a person be true to a mentality about riding or killing another black family, when you can build, and have more shit together. That's stupid shit! Then, when they get lock down, they do all kinds of shit to get out, which they call good behavior. But doing stupid shit to go in. Man nephew, it's enough money out here for everybody. Never forget that. If niggas would change their mindset about getting and having money they would always have some. Majority of our people want somebody to give them something. If you give somebody something that didn't cost them nothing, and they still have that same mentality of something for nothing mentality don't give them nothing or fall for that yokey-doke. Fuck'em!" I asked him, "How did you get yours? I mean what did you do to be a millionaire?" Mr. Sinclair, "Nephew, I'm not a millionaire. I just know how to use money. I like the finer things of life. When I was coming up with your father and Black Jack. We came up at a time when the game of money, women, hustlers, black business men had respect for one another. Have you read anything about "Black Wallstreet" in Oklahoma. Our people were living good back in the early 1900s. You know why they were able to live like millionaires, and some of them were millionaires?" I asked why, "Because they understood the vaule of a dollar, and how to use it. They also understood the empowerment of collective work. Today, everything and everybody is me, me, me and I, I, I. You rarely hear us, unless it's a close knit family, and some of them you can't even socialize with each other for the greater good. So, when I was out there running them streets. I was giving game from a cat called, "Too Clean." Man could that guy dress. He always wore a two-piece suit. He told me Youngblood, if you want to be respected, then get some money. Then dress and act like you got money, then you will have some money. Everytime you get a quarter, save that quarter, and go back and do the same thing you did to get that quarter, and repeat the process, then you will have a dollar, then repeat that process to get another dollar. If you do that for years you will be a rich man one day. Then, he told me, if you let your qurater and dollars grow, then you will see that magic of money, and you will hear and see the most powerful converstaion that a man can have. You know what he was talking about nephew?" I replied, "No, I can't say I do." He said, "That's where the old saying comes from, "*That money talks, and bullshit walks.*" Our people don't know how to listen to money, when they see or have the money, they run off spending it faster than they can come up with a plan to have more. When I was shining shoes, and running errands for them old school cats they were laying bread and game down on me. I was making more money than my parents, even though I left home early. "Too Clean" was sharp and good with numbers. He told me to read my Bible. He said what most black people didn't understand is that the Bible is a money book or economical book. But the religion has made them niggas dumb and blind. They don't know what to do with money. Plus, they was taught all that bullshit from those mistranslations bullshit in the Book, "that the love of money is the root all evil." Niggas are so blind they can't see, it's that lack of money that got niggas out there robbing and killing because they are trying to get their hands on some money. "*It's the lack of having money and not loving money it's the root of all evil.*" Because if every nigga had a million dollars he would be out spending, and not robbing and killing for it, because he would have it. Since our people don't know the language of money, that's why they don't know the power of money. They hear these sayings and streets philosophy about money, they lose control because they fail to understand when someone that knows the language of money says that money is powerful, usually they have money. Nephew do you know what makes money so powerful?" I replied, "No I do not." Old School went on, "The thing that makes money powerful is, what the money can do, and the powerful mental determination it takes to get real money, and always have some money. And to get to this point you have to be disciplined. No one can be strong in anything unless that person has discipline. Anyone without money is a person without discipline. If you keep giving them money, basically you are throwing money out the window. And being in a rush to spend it, is a person without money. So nephew, you want something to drink." While Mr. Sinclair step back into the house to snatch him and I something to drink. I was sitting there thinking about everything I heard about getting money, and keeping money. I know the universe put me in this situation to be here, and to listen to someone speak about money, discipline, gains, getting wisdom, and being successful. Melody asked her father, "Was Mr. Sinclair a millionaire?" Her father stated, "Depending on how you look at it. Her mother and herself looked like I'm confused, and then she commented, "What I'm saying is that, most people that tell you about money usually don't have any. Like the same people that have bad relationships-always telling other people on how to have one. You know what I'm saying?" Carlo smiled at his daughter, and he was shocked from her comment. He knew she was smart, but that statement really made him a proud father. He always taught his daughter to never waste her time talking to someone that didn't put their words into action. Or listening to people that love to talked about anything that didn't have real substance. Carlo went into a well constructive spiel, " Baby-girl you have to realize Mr. Sinclair is up in age at that time, but he's still sharp. His mind doesn't move like it use to when he was younger, and we all will go through it, if some of us live long enough. Plus, he told me he just wanted to be financially free or comfortable. That was his goal, so that's why he's living the way he is living. No, he isn't a millionaire far as dollar amount, but he's a millionaire if he tally up his owned assests. My desire and goal was to be a millionaire. That desire burned within me so deeply- it kept me up many nights. This desire to be a millionaire was all that I saw, dreamt about, visioned, and ever wanted to achieve. It just brings to mind two powerful statements of wise words from the Bible." After being silent for a while he wife asked, "Which Bible verse is that?" Carlo "The Wiz" reiterated, "Come on baby, we been through this topic before. You asked me that same question before. I know you were a devoted Baptist." Carlo chuckled and laughed very hard. His daughter thought she missed something. When it came to religious people's thoughts, and their power of reasoning, it was so illogical to her father. It would always tickle him, but majority of the time he just kept it to himself. He didn't want to hurt anyone's feelings concerning their faith or belief system. Melody bellowed, "Did I miss something?" Carlo was trying to answer his daughter's question, but he was laughing so hard from that superb-herb it made it difficult for him to speak. His stomach and side was hurting from laughing so hard he continued with the lessons on how to go from valley low and broke, to mountain high of millions. " Check this out baby-girl. The Good Book says, *'What a man thinks in his heart so is he,'* and it also says, *'A person or people without a vision will perish.'* Meaning that whatever dominates a peron's thoughts majority of the time will become that person's actions, and if the pereson don't have a goal for a higher or better life, will die in that state of mentally depressed, spiritually weak, and physically sick state. That's why our people are in destitute states of being day in and day out, and fooling themselves that we are making progress. Melody stated, " Basically, father you are saying that our minds and thoughts is the hallmark of everything we do, and what we will get out of life?" His wife and his eyes locked, and then his wife said, "Well Wiz!" Carlo shook his head in agreement with his daughter, and went on, " See baby-girl I.. He was cut off by his daughter's question, "Mom why you called dad Wiz? I heard you say that numerous of times, but I never knew why. Can you tell me why?" Her mother replied, "Your father his going to tell you why everyone that we know, why they call him by that name. He's going to tell you why they call him that." Carlo went on, " Yes baby-girl you will know why. When a person or people are morally and spiritually bankrupt, so will their bank account and pocket book will be nothing." That last statement that her father stated was right on the money when it came to Meoldy's husband. He was spiritually and mentally bankrupt. He was angry at the world, that he quit his only job when Meoldy and him first began to date. Meoldy tried everything to get her husband to snap out of his depression, self-pity and blame game. One thing we know that any person that encounter this type of breakdown will and can not accomplish anything. He would blame her when she stood by his side, but anger mixed with blame is blindness, which means no one can see the light of the truth if it slapped them in the face. He blamed his parents for being poor, he blamed the white people for their hypocrisy of justice and so-called opportunity. He blamed his job for paying him low-wages hourly. He blamed the politicians for legislating imbalance and unfair laws, and he blamed the preachers for ripping off the poor and undeducted masses for their hard earn money. When Meoldy's husband snapped out of it, she was so happy. She always believed that her father's strong disposition was the major reason that her husband got his act together.

"Mr. Sinclair spoke these words of wsidom, and from the very first time I heard those words, they became the hallmark of my living philosophy and money conscious perspectives. Melody chimed in, "So father what are those words that played a great part of your life?" Carlo "The Wiz" hung around wise street cats, that he became an old man of mind, but a young man physically. Carlo answered his sweet lovely daughter's undying question, that made her jumped with inner excitement. "He said, if a man doesn't aim for something in life," his daughter interrupted thinking she knew the rest of the quote. Like the whole world are stuck to that old saying, *'that if you don't stand for something you will fall for any and everything.'* Carlo laughed, and his wife was smiling gracefully. She knew her husband had his own philosophy about life, and that he didn't stick to the new school rules, which were made by damn fools. That one thing she learned quickly about her husband when they first dated. He always had a new quote with a deep philosophical thought, with mind provoking connotations. "No, baby-girl, he said if man doesn't aim for something in life, that man don't have anything to gain, but mental and spiritual pain and blame. Which only leads to anger and hatred for anything and everybody that's doing good. If a man truly desires to be successful, he must overcome his internal hurdles that appears to be too high or too deep to cross. It's only his warped conception, that gives him that same perception in his physical form. But majority of the people fail to realize this, so they stay stuck in their blame, anger, hatred, envy, jealousy and broke petty lives." Mrs. Rodgers posed a serious question for her husband, "So, honey did Merci, whatever her name is. Did she ever tried to come on to you? Or better yet, did she ever try to get close to you? You said you kept it professional, but did she keep it that way or what?" Once again, Carlo "The Wiz" stuck to the old script. Keep a lid on the game, when the cards are dealt from the bottom. He never told his wife the truth about Merci and him. Not only did she live there for free, she became Carlo's woman, and she started giving him half of her money that she made that nights she was dancing. She got so hooked to Carlo he had to pull a rabbit out of his hat to get rid of her, when she became too possessive. One night after they had their sexual merry-go around, and Merci slept later than usual. Carlo "The Wiz" got up early, and left home. He went to the corner store, and called the home office, making sure that Merci wouldn't receive the phone calls. After calling three times, he came home with two cups of coffee. He called Merci several times, she was sleep talking, and not fully awake. Carlo shook her, and asked her again were there any phone calls. She said she didn't know. Carlo went to the room where the office phone was sitting on the desk, and pushed the button for the answer machine. He made sure the volume was loud enough for Merci to hear. She jumped out of bed running toward the office, when she heard the messages. Carlo was standing behind the desk with his arms folded with a facial expression of anger, when she entered the office. It was all according to his plans. Carlo was determined by all means to reach his goal. Every time he had a set-back or temporary failure, he would think of his father. And that would fuel his ambition to not let his father down. He remembers one night when his father and himself were smoking some superb-herb, and his father spoke some words of wisdom. *'Son many of our people, and people in general would say that the mind is a powerful thing, and knowledge is power. But how many of them every put their mind to the test to see how powerful their mind really is. My son, let me break something down for you. The mind is powerful whether its destructive or constructive. So, when you see our people in their everyday condition of living, which is a struggling day in, and day out. What you see is a powerful destructive mind at work. And that destruction starts first with that person! Son, be very careful with your thoughts, your friends, your money and habits that you may develop consciously or unconsciously. If you live a poor life of poverty, that only means you have a poor skull game, and the only thing you can and will reap is poverty. This life gives you what you put in to it. For example, if you live by the gun, you will die by the gun. If you live to get money, you will get money. If love to gossip, then gossip which always leads to an emotional mess, then emotional mess is all you will get, you dig? I don't want you to struggle like I had too. By there is one thing that I always been proud of myself for, and that was the day I received the papers that my home was paid for. That was my focus, so that's what I achieved. And your mother was so happy, that it made me the happiest man in the world. Don't forget what I'm telling you. Your Pops love you man.'* Carlo was all business. He used three of the workers at the corner store to call his business phone. They were acting like they were business connections.

Carlo paid them $50 each to keep their mouths shut about the situation. Merci, jumped out of the bed. She starting apologizing about missing the calls. Until this very day she still feels guilty about losing and letting down the man that she loved, admired and the man that helped her achieve her nursing degree. Even though she is living the good life, and helping her sister and her nieces and nephews live better. There's not a day that goes by when she just ponders, wonders and sometimes shed a tear or two about the man she loved so dearly. She wanted to be Carlo's woman for life, because of his intelligence, discipline and caring side that she saw, which entails that he would help with no strings attached. Merci still believes that until this very day, that she was the reason her relationship didn't work out with Carlo. She still blames herself for not getting out of bed early, knowing that the man she wanted was all business, and sleeping was never a trait or excuse to over look business. Carlo "The Wiz" played his game so smoothly. He only did this because Merci was getting to emotional, and love was in her eyes, and coming out her ears. She was smart, but green. She was beautiful, but a L-seven. His mind was on being a millionaire, and if that meant breaking hearts, losing so-call friendships or being considered selfish, then so be it. Carlo stuck to his life lesson that he learned, which is, _"it's always better to have money, and need money and not have money when you need it."_ Carlo told his wife exactly what she wanted to hear, and needed to hear, "My only Sunshine, that girl was out of my league, and I needed her, and she needed me. We both were trying to achieve something. I made sure that girl got her nursing degree." Mr. Rodgers asked, "Well did she get it?" Carlo replied, "Hell yeah, she got it!" Then she spoke again, "So, how did you get rid of her?" Carlo learned that it's imperative that any business person or street hustler must learn the art of thinking fast on your feet. He came back, " I went to her graduation, and afterwards we went out for dinner. We talked about our plans. She had a job offer in another state, and from that night I never seen or talk with her again." Carlo didn't tell his wife, that Merci would called him all the time, but he would never answer her call anyway. He did what he told her, and he stuck to it. Even though deep down, Merci was one beautiful young woman. She was so beautiful, it was like if you touched her physically too hard, you would break her God-given mode. Merci appeared like the most hypnotic illusion in the physical world, that man's eyes couldn't believe what they saw, when they laid eyes upon her. His wife was also beautiful and flawless, but Merci was so hot! She was so hot she could steal the heat from fire. She was smoking! Carlo totally understood why "Cat-Daddy"did what he could to keep her dancing. She was a real money maker, because of her beautiful God-given mode. But she was too smart to remain dumb, when it came to sticking to her plans, and putting those plans to work. Plans that are made have to be fulfilled by all means, if not, then what's the reason for making them in the first place.

The Money Game

As the sun begin to set, the family were still enjoying each others time and company. Life has proving to those that truly understand, and able to see. When love is truly in the atmosphere of couples or people, time is not an issue whatsoever. Sweet Melody jibed to her father, "So daddy, you still haven't said how and what you did to become rich." Carlo throw up his hands in a surrendering gesture with a big smile on his copper-tone face. He spoke with great enthusiasm, "Well, about a month or two later, I had a empty rental property and money was getting low, and them damn pink slips were back in cycle again. Oh, before I forget! When I was cleaning up the mess I made when Merci packed her stuff. I opened the desk drawer, there was an envelope inside the drawer. It was $2000 inside the envelope. Plus, there was a letter she had written also. Remember when I stormed out of the house, and left, Merci was still at the house. It was hours later when I got back, and she was gone." Carlo's wife asked, "What did the letter say?" Carlo quickly and mentally gather his thoughts together. He understood how the minds and emotions operate from a female perspective. He conducted his words exactly the way his wife needed to hear them. Carlo said,

" It said something like…huh, I can't remember totally word for word. It said something like, *'Dear Carlo, I am very sorry that I let you down. I truly apologize for missing those much needed phone calls. I know how much you are trying to fulfill your vision or goals of being a millionaire, and business contacts is a major part of that vision. You kept your word about helping my sister and me. I love you so dearly! I know you know that, because you are a very intelligent man. I hate to admit this, but I think you was one of the most intelligent person I ever known. I mean this dearly and honestly your intelligence is greater than my dad. My father is a very stubborn man, verses your discipline with clarity and great logic.* Carlo paused for a second. His wife asked again, "What's wrong honey?" Carlo replied, " I'm trying to remember, oh okay! She also wrote, *'To not be near you, see you, and talk with you hurts greatly. As I write this, I hope the paper doesn't be to wet from the tears that constantly pours from my eyes as I write this. You was all I wanted in a man, and I messed that up for over sleeping, knowing my responsibility. I knew that taking phone calls was my duty, and I screwed up. I hope you take it into your heart, and forgive me. You were honest and straight forward about taking care of your business. I still remember that handsome strong facial expression written on your face, 'we got to play this game airtight,' but I wasn't. If you ever find it in your heart to forgive me, you know where to find me. I sincerely and honestly pray that you do forgive and find me. I hope you find a way through that intelligent mind of yours to let me back into your life, and I also left something for you. Since, it was my fault that those important calls were missed. So, I feel compelled to leave you some money, even though those phone calls could have been worth more or probably they were some rich influential people. I love you so much, you are like air to me. Take care of yourself . Love you very much Merci."*

"I took that money, and put it back into desk, and thought of my next move. Melody emotions was getting the best of her from that letter, "Father, that girl was deeply in love with you. And until this very day you haven't heard or spoke to her?" Carlo answered, " No I haven't! Baby-girl when I'm done with certain people, I am done! It's no going back plain and simple. Anyway, while sitting at the desk. The phone ranged it was Mr. Bernstein, informing me to come to his office. My money was getting low like a said before, and everything that I was planning wasn't working according to the plans I was making. I couldn't stop or give up, that shit is not in my blood, you dig? I rarely was talking with Black Jack. He was suffering from pancreatic cancer at the time, and on top of that Mr. Sinclair was back and forth to the hospital. He was suffering from a stroke. But I was still getting info, and the low down that I needed mentally to stay focus. These men were like father-figures to me, and they taught me numerous of things, because they believed in me. When I arrived at Mr. Bernstein's office he hit me for $2000 this time, and he gave me an address for a social networking party they have every year. At least that's what he told me. Mr. Bernstein told me, 'There will be some hard-nose serious men there. These men are all business when it comes to money. So, I would suggest you polish yourself up. I'm giving you the opportunity to make something happening in your favor. I'll do what I can to help, but majority of this shit is up to you, excuse my French! I'll still remain your lawyer, when you need my service." He wrote the address and time of the gathering down on back of one of his business card. I was back riding the bus. It's a good thing he didn't follow me out to the parking garage. He was already convinced that I had a car. I rode the bus back down to rental car office. They didn't have the same black Jaguar. They had a luxury Lincoln, and that was the closet I was going to get to a money car. Plus, I had my story covered if he asked what happen to the Jag." Mrs. Rogers chimed in, "You was going to tell him it was in the shop." Carlo shook his in agreement, and replied, " You know it!"

"Two weeks flew by, and it was the night to use street game if it came down to it, which is a means of leverage. When I got out of the big body Lincoln, with a $1000 in my pocket, which isn't nothing to these people. I stormed on in, and stood for a second. I looked around-then headed for the bar. It was maybe about one-hundred people or so. I received my drink from the bartender, and moments later Mr. Bernstein was coming through one of the side glass door. When he approached me, we shook hands. I followed him back through the same glass door. There were four men standing outside smoking cigars. I shook hands with all of them, and we all introduced ourselves. I stood there listening to these guys talk about business. One yellow head tall guy asked me what business I was in, I told him real estate. He said I quote, "That's a good business to be in boy. Not everybody can be prosperous in that business.' I was about to lose my cool, when he called me boy. I stuck to the script, and plus I had invested to much money to walk away with nothing. One short brown head pop-belly fellow, that looked like his belly was about to fall to the ground because he was so short. He said with a whining voice, " Excuse me, what's your name again?" Carlo I said, he responded, "Okay. Franchise is the business to get into, it's basically real estate, but most people thinks it's a food business. Food is the reason for the business or building to conduct the business. It stills boils down to location, location, location. Maybe you can talk with Brenda my ex-wife. Maybe she can give you a few pointers on the business." One grey eyed white headed skinny fellow bellowed, "He's not into franchising! He's into real estate dealing with homes." The guy that spoke first replied to the white-headed guy, "It's still the same. See Carlo, I told you. That's why most people can't be successful, because they don't know what business they are into." There was a medium height guy with a shaved head, wearing some glasses and he spoke, " To be a great investor in the business world, is to understand first and foremost, is that when you first start a business it's like a jig-saw puzzle. It's many pieces in the beginning to be solved, but you have to start with something for all the other pieces to come together. Sometime you try to match a piece that appears to fit, but it doesn't. Then, you realize that one doesn't work, so you try another piece, and it doesn't work. At some point in time, you start to doubt or wonder did I really wanted to start this endeavor or project. If you can make it through all your self-doubt, and continue on the journey you decided to start. It's like that completed jig-saw puzzle. Beautifully completed with great adoration, which is the reward or payoff for sticking through all the chaos. And all of that self challenging is nothing but disguised order and reward. But it shapes and molds you to become the very thing you want. Most people don't understand that! What is actually happening, is that you are creating a vessel for you to obtain what you wish to have. Does that make sense to you? Mr. Bernstein told me you were a serious man, that's looking to invest into stock or whatever. My name is Warren Wiener. Whenever you are ready let me know, and here's my card." We shook hands again. A this sandy hair guy said, "My name is Paul. Warren is a very shrewd and smart businessman. That's why he's a millionaire." They all laughed. Warren replied, "I am not a millionaire!" Paul cut in, "He doesn't like to admit it. But he is! Don't let him fool you. All kidding aside, having a successful business or making some serious money, is loving what you do, solving people problems or having an idea, and sticking with that idea in order to capitalize on it. You got to have some serious passion about being successful in order to be successful one day." Melody asked her father, "What was going through your mind when you were hearing all that stuff, and the guy that called you boy?" Carlo answered his daughter, "Baby-girl, I had to over look that statement, and listening to all this information that was greatly overwhelming and inspirational. Anyway, the yellow head guy that called me boy his name was Jacob Swenson. We all went back in, and headed back to the bar for another drink. "I had to get my game together."

"So, I started going back to the Foxx Inn Lounge, and I met this chick name "Satin." That was her stage name, and she was trying to make a move on me. Then, she was trying to get hip to what Merci and I had at the time. She said that Merci didn't work there anymore. She also told me that Cat-Daddy was doing time for drugs and pimping and pandering. They gave him 65 years, but then they find out that the girl was using a fake ID card portraying to be twenty when she was actually sixteen. So, his charges were dropped to 40 years. While sitting there rapping with "Satin" with her wide hips and red-helium blown thighs. I asked her have she seen Spoons. When she responded, as the saying goes 'speak of the devil and he will appear. Spoons had just walked in when I popped that question. He came over, and right off the back he started drilling me with negative shit, but that was my nigga. He said I quote, "How is that million dollar corporation going?" Satin was still sitting there when he popped that question. She looked and cracked a mischievous smile with an expression, I am at the right place at the right time, was written all over her face. Not knowing, that I was broker than three dope-fiends and two desperate hookers. Spoons negativity did something, and one of the comments he made drilled deeply within my mind." His daughter asked, "What did he say?" Carlo replied, "He said nigga, ain't no hood nigga goin to make it in that white man's world of business. So, you can quit with all that dreaming, and wake your ass up to what's really happening. Nigga you were born a street hustler, your old man was a street hustler, and that's all we know is this street shit. So stop wasting your fucking time. I don't meant to come at you like that. But I just got to keep it one-hundred with you!" He bought us a few rounds of cognac, and then I split the scene. That next morning I went to the bank cause I had copped a blue-sheet that listed all the homes, cars and small business that people were selling. I used one of my empty rental property for collateral, and bought a home that was worth more than my rental property that was in foreclosure. Then, I came across this guy that was selling one of his five Laundromats. He sold it for $5000, and told me that it generated about $3000 to $4000 a month. I bought it. When it came to the foreclosed home I had to put some work into that foreclosed home. I couldn't sleep for nights. I was fired up that morning. I had to make this shit happening. I got "Bulldog" that's Mr. Sinclair's lawyer on the horn. I asked if he knew of some rich powerful black people I could meet with. He laughed, and said "I guess you ready to see how some of us black people can make some money moves ourselves. Come on by my office in about two hours, and we can go see a close friend of mines. Plus, he's a millionaire. That's what you want to hear right?" He knew I did."

"Those two hours felt like eternity. I met with this guy name Clarence Mitchell he was the CEO of "Mitchell and Brown Private Equity Firm. He said the business manage about $300 million dollars. That is one thing he shouldn't have not made mention." Mrs. Rogers commented, "That's when you told me that he hated or didn't like Harry Belmar?" Carlo stated, "He told me that Mr. Belmar money management firm was managing like $600 million dollars. When I found out that he didn't like Mr. Belmar. I told him I met with the old fellow, and he was going to cut me on a good investment with his firm for little or nothing. And he said you were a cheapskate. I just lied, but I was using that as my leverage, and I told Mr. Belmar the same thing I told Mr. Mitchell. I told Mr. Clarence Mitchell, man you and Mr. Belmar are worse than the niggas on the street. I would think you and him would be more incline to do business together to become bigger and better. So what I did was started flipping houses, and making profits, and using the bank's money or other people's money. There were times when I had to hold the homes longer than I wanted too, but has long as I had the money, I did it." Mrs. Rodgers asked, "You didn't say what happened that night at the networking party." Carlo hesitated for a moment, then continued, "I met Jacob's ex-wife Brenda, and I used that mental twist on her. I told her some shit that her ex-husband didn't say, just to get under her skin to see where she was mentally. I told her that Jacob said she was a tired and lazy fuck, and that she hated black people. She turned red as the blood running through my arteries. The bartender gave her another drink. We sat at the bar drinking and talking. She gave me her card, and also her address to her home. I insisted that she keep her home address to herself. And she blurted, "Oh, so you think I'm prejudice too, huh. So you were out there believing all that shit. That spoil bastard makes me sick! Let me tell you something, that no good sonuvabitch was born rich. That cocksucker was fucking every secretary he hired. I was working late one night at the office. I slept at the office, and called home and his cell phone, and I never got an answer. That next morning everyone was at work except for him and our secretary. So I drove home, and he wasn't there, then I went to one of our corporate homes that we use for functions like this, and it's a way to get a tax cut. And there they were naked as the day they came into this world. They were so loaded from drinking and boozing all night. They didn't hear the door chime, after I turned off the alarm, and yelled and screamed. Then I stormed out of the house. Angry of course! I sued his ass, and divorced him. I must admit, he did help me get establish. What most people fail to realize is all the shit that no good bastard put me through. I took that money, and invested into nine franchises." I chimed in, "So what's your net worth, if I may ask?" Brenda looked at me like how dare this sonuvabitch ask me that, but she said, "About average annually 2.5 million dollars. To invest in a franchise you will need about $300,000 for one store, and that's to cover you for a least 1 to 2 years, because I know you know that the average business fails within the first or second year, and some struggle with the third year. If your business can make it pass the third year you are in good shape."

"I pondered on that information for weeks. I thought I made another mistake until I read over several investment books several times. I realized that when I took a loan out, and used my empty rental property for collateral, which turned out to be an asset. I used that loan as a good debt to turn into an assets, only because I invested the money to put more money back in my pockets. That's what the game of money is all about knowing how to use it, and keep it, to become free from debt, or trading physical labor for a few dollars that will never make you truly rich or wealthy. I paid the money back, and sat down with Mr. Belmar, and bought 10,000 shares, which means that I owned 1% of the company, and went to Clarence Mitchell's firm and did the same thing. I was owner of big money making firms. Even though I only owned 2%. I went down Flip Street to Ms. Vera's where they gambled, played porker, spades, dominoes and shot craps. Ms. Vera was an appealing yellow bone. She was slim and her ass was big and square like a box and flat as ever. She was still appealing I must admit. Her hair was braided so neatly that it looked like a beautiful beehive. Every time she would smiled that gold tooth would light up her face. She was an old sexy woman for her age. She wasn't afraid to tell you her age either. A fifty-five year old woman looking like she was thirty-five, damn she was a sexy old lady. I used every trick that Black Jack taught me, when it was all said and done. I left Ms. Vera's with $2200 in my pocket. Before making it out the door, I slid Ms. Vera $100 bill. She winked her eye at me, and put the bill in her bra. As soon as I jumped in the car, and spit out the small green dice that I had in my mouth. The fucking Rollers rolled up on me. The suckas told me they had a warrant out for my arrest damn near five fucking years. The charge was for aggravated assault with a deadly weapon. That shit went all the way back, when I had that altercation with the guy at the gas station. Right when everything was looking up. Melody asked her father, "How long did you stay in jail?" Carlo replied, "I called Mr. Bernstein, and was out in the next three days, and had to appear in court but it was thrown out. The prosecutor had no evidence of a weapon, so the judge tossed out the case. I took $3,500 an opened up good growth-mutual fund for 10 years long investment strategy. It was a bumpy road on the way, but I stuck with it. A ten year investment at 5.5% interest yearly for ten years you do the math, and dumping $200 into it every month. I still wasn't done. I met with Mr. Belmar and Clarence, to see if I could be a partner in their investment firms, knowing that I already owned 1% in each of their firms. I wanted more money, and more leverage. I was told that if I could make a larger investments or work inside the firm generating more money for the firm, basically bring in more clientele I would able to make more money. So, I got Brenda Swenson to invest with Mr. Belmar and Mr. Bernstein to invest with Mr. Mitchell. Even though he was apprehensive at first, but he gave in. He didn't think blacks know anything about big money investing. Brenda and I was becoming closer. Mrs. Rodgers chimes in, "What you mean you and her was becoming closer? Basically, you saying that you slept with her." Carlo was tired of the sugar-coating shit, "Hell yes, I slept with her! It was part of my strategy and plan." His daughter asked, "What kind of strategy dad?" His wife also bellowed, "How can you sleep with the enemy? They are the same people that murder our people, police shoot are young kids down everyday, worse than that they put dogs on us, they raped our people, put high pressure water hoses on our people. I mean how can you? A man of your caliber, and plus you didn't tell me everything. You told me you dealt with women on a business level. I think you enjoyed being with that white woman. Carlo "The Wiz" replied, "If I did enjoy being with that woman, they way you speak on it. You and I wouldn't be husband and wife today, dig that! Plus, I told you years ago, that was a strategy, and you said you understood that I had to do what I had to do. Since, you been sipping on that wine your ass is slipping and tripping. Like I said, when it comes to women, ya'll emotion takes charge, until you feel used, abused and neglected. When that happens, that's when women will use their intellect. What I was doing was getting Brenda hooked on me emotionally. I wanted her to fall for me deeply, and then she would do anything for me, which any woman that's deeply in love will do for any man. So, yes

I slept with her, and it all paid off in the long run. I needed those franchise investments. I staged up a little heist. I setup a dinner where Brenda. Mrs. Rogers raised her voice with, "You didn't tell me about no heist or some type of setup!" Carlo thought to himself, shit am I'm being too honest, and that's not how I achieved my riches. I was only truthful to myself, not other people. But this is my family. He went on, "Well it went like this, plus I did what the fuck I had too. All the shit is in the fucking past, and we all living good now. So what's the damn problem?" Melody spoke and her voice was shaking and cracking, "I think I better go home." Carlo shook his head, and looked at his beautiful wife, and said, " I apologize, and I will go ahead a make this short and sweet, ok.?" Melody shook her head. She never seen her father get that angry. He always displayed a cool and calm demeanor. She thought that's how my father became rich. He's a ruthless operator. One thing she knew from watching mafia movies with her husband, and she was convinced that ruthlessness is what all serious streets dudes must use to survive, and make some serious money. Carlo said, "Anyway I got Spoons to hook me up with "K-Bill" off Flip Street, to print up some counterfeit money. "K-Bill" was light, bright with nigga fight. He was a mix breed. That was reared in the hood. His mother was black and father was a white ex-Navy Seal. He knew technology heavily. He stood about six feet even with spots of dark brown speckles on his face. This cat could sit at a computer for hours and hours, but he made some serious bread with that computer. That's what the damn computer was created for, take make money domestically or internationally. I had him print up what looked like $50,000. I drove out to Brenda's condo, and parked on Bella and Kingston Blvd. I had Spoons and Satin pulled the jack. They was going to rob Brenda and me. But first, I had to get her to open her purse to see what she had that was worth the jack, and then after all we were kicking it pretty tough, and that was a way to get her to fell guilty, about $50,000 which she didn't know that was fake. So, in return she would give $50,000 in real cash or grant me a franchise. Either way the shit had to happen. Weeks before we went out. I had to search for a spot to pull off the jack, you dig? It was a place called the Cocktail Palace. No baseball caps, no T-shirt or tennis shoes were allowed. I drove to Brenda's condo to pick her up for our dinner date. She buzzed me in, when I arrived, and stepped in the door, she was standing there in this large elegant living room naked. She was so thin I could have counted every rib on her naked body. I never did like thin women. I told her that I liked her very much, but that's what our relationship was all about. Anyway we went at it like raging dogs in heat. I knew she liked rough sex. After a rough quickie. She jumped in the shower. While she was getting dress, I was standing their with an express of admiration and delight on my face. Internally that wasn't the case at all. She put on a black night dress, no under wear, no bra, then she put on some very expensive diamond earrings, and a expensive watch to go along with that big diamond ring she wore. She sprayed some perfume on her that filled the room with a sweet scent, that seem to move along gracefully. Even though she was divorced she still wore her ring. She looked at me and said, " I don't wear underwear!" We were headed out the door when the phone ranged. She pushed the speaker and her ex-husband Jacob Swenson was on the horn screaming, "Brenda, I heard that you been around town with that fucking nigger, Carlo! I know he's probably there now! Brenda yelled back at him, "Get a fucking life!" She pushed the button on Jacob, and while we were stepping out the door, the phone ranged again. I popped her on the ass. She ran back in, and removed some items from one purse to put in her small black purse. She told me when you are rich, you can do what you want when you want. She walked up to me and kissed me, and said, 'I will make sure you live this life like you should or should I say we deserve.' I told her damn you look so appealing, you make me want some more of that good stuff. I tapped her on that little round ass again. I must admit she wasn't flat, but she was thin."

"About thirty to forty-five minutes later we arrived at the restaurant. She awe struck, when we arrived to the spot to dine. We sat there making small talk before ordering our dinner. When we finished eating, and talking about business, relationships and sex and all types of other shit. After we ate dinner I pulled out my wallet to pay, but she insisted. I saw some cash, but I really couldn't see the total amount. Those diamond earrings and watch had me playing the appraisal. I know I was looking at about $50 to $100,000 or more. I excused myself, and went to the restroom, and told them the plan was still on. Remember to use fake tattoos to be seen, which can be used a personnel identity without showing their face. While sitting there, I told Brenda that I have $50,000 in cash to invest into one of her franchise or business, or some international stock investment. Brenda was elated, "You are serious about investing, and becoming rich?" I told her, " Hell yes. I gave her the two white envelopes stuffed with cash. I ordered another drink for us. I kept looking over to my left, and this woman just kept looking, and smiling at me. I was wondering what's the hell that's all about. She had blonde hair, with a wicked smile. She was swing her leg with heels back and forth, which indicated that she was horny. But I couldn't oblige her. She didn't look bad from what I saw of her. My mind was on what was getting ready to go down.

Brenda was speaking on the importance of a trained mind with goals, when she was interrupted. This guy was well dressed and tall, and appeared to be very prosperous. He had a woman with him, that looked has though she was a few years older than him. They both approached the table. He introduced himself, 'My name is Mark McCloud, and this is my beautiful fiancée Laura Winters. And I still have those papers for you, whenever you are ready to make the deal.' We shook hands. He stated before he left, 'Well you folks enjoy your evening.' Mark was a tall slender guy with gold cropped hair. He had raging blues eyes. He was dressed in a black sports-jackets, with some black loafers, with some black jeans, and his fiancée was wearing a red evening dress with red heels, and red small purse under her arm. She was also wearing some pearl earrings and necklace around her thin neck. Her brunette hair was cropped on her circular shape dome. I asked Brenda what business he was into? She told me he's a Wall Street trader for one of Wall Street's mega firms. Brenda went back to her initial conversation, 'Do you know the importance of reading, and why it's very imperative to read and stay focus. It's not easy. That's the reason many people don't become millionaires, because they can't stay focus long enough. Without discipline and being totally committed with all seriousness, success is unachievable. Plus, to reeducate yourself with a millionaire mentality with ambition, desire and drive is the hallmark of becoming successful. Without those traits, you can dream all you want, but nothing will happen until the mind and body makes the connection to act with conviction. Only then can you achieve the goal and the vision will manifest. When I got with Jacob, I had to educate myself on money, leadership, investing, management, the importance of goal setting, and going or listening to a business seminars once a week. I went to college, and got a degree in government affairs. Jacob told me I should have got a degree in technology or business. Oh well, he purchased numerous of books on business for our home. This guy's library is flowing with books on business, war, leadership, time management and people management, investing and economics. One thing I found out about people, is that you really don't know them until you lived with them or been with them for years. Five years after our marriage, that ass-hole showed me who he really was. So, I kept my marriage name, because of the economical doors that were opened for me. Plus, I had to put up with a lot of bullshit, while being married to that man. I figure I would get all that I deserved, so I kept my marriage name. That's why I am very well known by rich and wealthy people. If, you are going to be in this game of power, wealth and being rich. You better make a name for yourself. Another thing I want you to never forget. Is the bullshit, about doing what you love. Get that bullshit out of your consciousness, right now! Do what the fuck makes you lots of money, and then love the shit that made you rich, and repeat the process ten-thousand times if it continues to work. Because there are economical down-turns, or what they call bubble and bust. Ride that horse of fortune and prosperity until it waivers, and about that time many innovative people will come to you with many more money making ideas. Never forget that making money is a game of life, and to win you must be smart, shrewd, discipline and pragmatically decisive. I'm telling you because I want to see you make it, and I care about you very much. I know you know that." She raised her heels, and started fumbling between my legs, and arousing my rod. She told me to follow her to the ladies restroom. I followed her into the ladies restroom, and we went into one of the stalls, and went right into a rough sexual escapade.

After that, we went back to our seats, and order another martini. She said, "Anyway back to you. I saw that written all over your demeanor when I first saw you." I replied, " You saw what?" She stated, "Drive, ambition, focus and determination." I was like, "Really!" I knew what she was doing, which is to see how ambitious and daring I am. One of the hallmarks of becoming successful is possessing the spirit of ruthless ambition, is to do what the fuck you want to, when you want to. Power and Respect! One of the bedrock of money, success and affluence. If I possessed that means of fearlessness, which is the root of being unstoppable. After about fifteen minutes, I seen Spoons black chromed-out spaceship rolled by. She wrote a check, and we headed for the door. We were talking and laughing like everything was cool, and the sun had set hours ago. It was dark outside, and while walking to the car like everything was all good. Spoons and Satin jumped out from behind a parked car, next to where I had parked. The parking lot was in the back of the establishment. With a tall dim light pole in the center of the parking lot. They wore bandanas that concealed their mouth and nose, and baseball caps pulled down with dark sunglasses over their eyes. Spoon's wore a black T-shirt with black sweat pants, with fake big dollar sign tattoos on both forearms, and Satin wore a black miniskirt with two big tattoos on the front of her large thighs. I said to Spoons speaking like as though he was a stranger. In her eyes he had to be a stranger robbing us, "You are making a big mistake." That nigga Spoons hit me on the side of my head with the butt of that rod he was holding, and said, "Nigga don't make me blow your fucking head off. Don't waste my fucking time, give it up! I saw in that nigga's face some real raw deep shit. I was thinking, this niggas is playing the game way too fucking real. I hope he haven't flipped on me. That was my nigga, but I saw another side to this nigga. Brenda gave up her watch, earrings, the purse, and the fake $50,000 that I just gave her. I was acting like a nigga on a Hollywood screen. Standing there gasping for air, and holding my blood dripping knotted up head. They also took our cell phones. So, we ran back into the restaurant. The police were called, but there was nothing they could do. I had to use some dinner towel, to prevent blood from getting everywhere. The looked at the camera, but the footage was so fuzz and blurry. One because it was dark, and two the camera was 50 to 100 yards away from where I parked the ride intentionally. I remember they played that footage on the news for weeks. It never came back to haunt us. I was acting like I just lost my whole world. I told Brenda I just took out a loan for that money, and I used one of my rental properties as collateral, and the other $25,000 is what my father left me before he passed. I was sitting at the dinner table with tears in my eyes. I started blaming her for us meeting there. She apologized over and over again. She told me she was going to make it up to me. We left and checked into a expensive hotel."

"When we arrived at the room, we were sitting up in the bed talking, and then she pulled out her briefcase. She was reading over some papers, and signing some forms. I received a call from Spoons. I acted like it was a legit business call, I stated, "We can meet tomorrow at 11am at your office." When Spoons and I met, the next day. I was like man, "What the fuck you bust me in my skull with that piece for? That shit was unnecessary!" Spoons spieled, "Nigga, you know we had to make the shit look real!" Anyway, after getting off the phone with Spoons. Brenda got up and went into the restroom. I heard the shower running, and I saw some papers hanging out of her briefcase. I walked into the restroom. I started kissing her, and I stated "Hurry up." I went to the

117

bed, and popped open the case, and saw some papers. The forms read, "Lakoks OIL Ind., and balance showing that she owned 280,000 of shares, worth about $825,385 at average of $2.75 to $3.62. I said damn, this bitch is loaded, and I will be also. Brenda was getting very possessive, which was fucking with my mental state. Anyway, I wanted to make mention of oil investing to her, but that would be too obvious. Which means I am prying into her business. That would cause her to no longer trust me, so I didn't mention it."

"That next morning we went to her bank, and she gave me a cashier check for $75,000. She stated, "Here's your start on becoming rich." I made her feel so guilty, about that shit, which was my plan. After depositing the cashier check at my bank, I jetted to the car dealer-ship, and bought a Black 4-door BMW, and jumped back deeper into the game of making serious money. I also opened a REIT which is a real estate investment trust, that way I made money by investing in a group of properties, which means other people were doing the work, and making me money at the same time. So basically, that's what I was doing to become rich. I gave Spoons and Satin $5,000 a piece. Don't you know that dumb bitch Satin, came to me weeks later demanding, that I give her another five-g's or she was going to the authorities on what happen. That's why the dumb bitch is sitting in the pen now. They gave that dumb bitch 25 fucking years. I was questioned, but they looked at the footage again, even though it was fuzzy, they were able to see two people with their hands up. They even snatched a few cats up from different neighborhoods, and Brenda and I were called to see these cats in a line up. The thing that saved Spoons and me, was that Brenda was very well known. She pulled, and pressed to speak with the mayor, and the police commissioner, about the deputies that were making accusation about my involvement. Plus, detective Ron Spencer told us, and he didn't believe her because of her past record. Come to found out the bitch tried to sue numerous of companies several times in the past, and a private investigator was hired by several of these companies' attorneys. Which meant she couldn't be trusted. She was labeled a compulsive lair I thought to myself, damn! I wonder if Mr. Sinclair, knew that the bitch was a fraud and scheming phony, just waiting to get money out of him on some bullshit. So she was labeled a compulsive liar. I was happy that the detective didn't ask for her or me to go into the interrogation room. Plus, the dumb bitch signed a confession. They probably would have seen the bitch's reaction, and go a tip the bitch was telling the truth. But I thought about the ways of nature, and the way she works her powerful magic. That scandalous bitch agreed on the amount she would receive from the heist, and turn around with greed to press a nigga. She got what she deserve. Greed always at some point in time will come back to haunt that greedy muthafucka. Spoons was never questioned, and plus I dropped another $5,000 on my man. Mr. Bernstein handled everything. So I will say, having a plan, and sticking to it is the only way to become rich, if that is your plan. Knowing the difference between a liability and an asset. Shit, Brenda was an asset, that's because she owned assets, and knew how to takeout loans or use other people's money to become rich, which can be a liability if you don't know what you were doing to become rich. Using loans for investing is smart, but using loans to buy shit that's worthless and meaningless is a great debt, which is a great life back breaking liability. That's what poor minded people do. They buy worthless and meaningless shit, instead purchasing shit that can put money in their pockets. Both firms that I invested with, were making more money, and

I would buy more shares. It's all about investing. Brenda and I were taking trips to Paris seeking other possible opportunities and shopping. When were at the Mall one day, and this chic came over, and asked was I married, and was the lady I'm with is my wife. Brenda was in the ladies room. When she came out, and saw that chic and I rapping. She went ballistic, and security was called, and people were standing around staring. Damn the bitch was getting out of control with her jealousy insecurities. I remember telling Mr. Sinclair about that situation. Melody asked, "What did Mr. Sinclair think about that situation?" Carlo "The Wiz" stated, "He told me, my game is strong, and plus she has entered a different world that she ever experienced with a cat like you. She knows money is not going to hold you, and she is really unsure what will keep you down and around. That's why she's insecure. She feels and thinks that anyone can be the one that steals you away. And you only seen the tip of the iceberg." Mrs. Rodgers asked, "What did he mean by that?" Carlo "The Wiz" replied, "That her ship with me is going to sink, because she is loosing control of herself. Her emotions is getting the best of her. And I was getting sick of it. There are several ways in a nutshell on how you can become rich. Which is having a plan, and sticking to it."

"I used my street tricknology, ambition, my father's wisdom, being a loner with a millionaire mind, to take me from the streets to the millionaire seats. And that's exactly what I did. I sat with millionaires that had big ideals and large ideas about living a successful life by all means. You got to mingle with people that are prosperous, or keep working your plan until you are able to raise your money and profile in the game. It's all game! And you have to play to win, *not that bullshit about it's not all about winning, it's about how you play the game. I know you heard that bullshit before.*

Melody my love, don't ever take that bullshit philosophy, and make it yours. Results is the ways and the means, that you, your mother and I was able to live damn good. By playing to win. Only by determination and dedication can anyone make it to this status." Melody got up and kissed her father, "I love you so much daddy. You are the best dad in the whole world, and mom I know it wasn't easy. Love you. Mrs. Rodgers replied, "No, sugar it definitely wasn't easy, as the saying goes love conquers all. All my doubts were removed years ago. I must admit at times, my emotions did get the best of me concerning your father, and the man he is. Like every time we would go out to eat or to the movies, some woman would be staring at him, or trying to get his attention. All the while I'm there." Melody asked, "Mom, how do you feel, when that happens?" She replied, "Sometime you don't like it because it's disrespectful, but then again I know my husband is a very handsome man, and his demeanor or the way he walks into a place, he displays confident without him saying anything. Plus, if someone doesn't want what you have, then probably you don't have anything worthy or valuable." Melody posed the same question to her father, "So dad, does that happen with you concerning mom. Do men try to hit on mom when you around?" Carlo smiled with that devilish grin and said "Mainly it happens when I'm not around. Like for instant, we were at the gas station. I was pumping gas. Your mother went into the store to pay for the gas, and get herself something to drink. I saw her put her finger up in this guy's face, and pointed at me sitting in the car." Mrs. Rodgers, "Oh yes, I remember that. He asked me, Ms. Foxy, are you married? I told him happily, and that's when he was following me out the door. So, I stopped and showed him my ring, and I pointed at your father. Life is beautiful, if you can see beauty in it."

The Front Porch

Melody asked her father, "How many homes do you have now?" Carlo "The Wiz" replied, "Well, baby-girl I have about ten homes, two franchises still in good operation. I also have a few investments with small oil companies. I also have a small lot that holds about fifty parked cars, which is next to the club Zoom. I give some of the guys that work for me, a chance to make some extra money. Sometimes, I go to the university or junior colleges, to see if some guys want to make money, and if they can be out late, and handle themselves. If so, hey have a job. I had three Laundromats, but sold two of them, and kept the one. I still have investments with two private equity firms." Mrs. Rodgers asked, "Do you ever see any of these people?" Carlo "The Wiz" answered, "Spoons is paralyzed now." Melody bellowed, "Why! What happen?" Her father stated, "Well there are many conflicting stories on what happened. Some say he got shot making a deal, some say he was at the club, and got caught in the cross fire. I never have asked him about what happen. That's my nigga! Even though Mr. Sinclair told me several times to stay away from Spoons. He had a rap sheet longer than my arm. He felt like Spoons was going to mess up my opportunity to fulfill my vision. Mr. Sinclair and Black Jack died years ago. That was some hard times for me, when those two men died." Carlo "The Wiz" eyes began to water up. He excused himself, and went to the restroom to compose himself. He came back out on to the porch. Carlo stated, "It was like losing my grandfather and father at one time. His granddaughter sold the club, and moved back to the Big Easy." Mrs. Rogers, "What happen to Brenda?" Carlo replied, "She died of cancer years ago also. I got served to be in court by that bitch's lawyer before she died. That bitch tried to sue me for all the shit she bought or done for me!" Melody chimed in, "Why did she do that." Carlo "The Wiz" took a breath and spoke, "When I told her I'm done with this relationship. She didn't want to end it. In the process, I countered sued her ass for time of miss work due her harassment and following me, making threats, slandering of my business, and scaring off my costumers, and she wrecked my car. Melody asked, "She drove your car?" Carlo "The Wiz" said, "No, I was sitting in the restaurant, and that bitch just ran her Mercedes into my BMW. I took a picture of it, and plus it was on the camera from the restaurant. That tape was played in court. I used Nicholas "Bulldog" Williams to represent me. That nigga is a bulldog for real in that courtroom. The judge made her pay me $1.5 million for slander, emotional disturbance, and damage to my property." Mrs. Rodgers, "What ever happened to the attorney you had at first?" Carlo answered, "Mr. Bernstein stopped practicing law, after he found out that he had some skin cancer. Mr. Belmar retired years ago. Who would ever believe that him and Mr. Clarence Mitchell eventually emerge firms, and expanded the firm. Melody asked, "Where did you, and mother meet?" Carlo "The Wiz" replied, "At the local bookstore, and we have been together every since that first moment. I know she was going to be my wife, because of her intelligence, her beauty and lady-like character and mannerism." Melody posed a question to her mother, "Did you know he was going to be your husband?" Her mother answered, "Of course, because of the way he carried himself, and the way he thinks, is very compelling and deeply effective. He moves you to act or prove yourself without him making it known to you that's what he shaping your inner being to doing." Melody got up and stretched and hugged and kissed her parents good-night. Then, headed to her coupe and jumped in and left.

Mr. and Mrs. Rodgers both jumped in the shower, and in the bed naked after drying off. It all started with passionate kissing, which led to making mad passionate love. When his wife reached her climax, she yelled, "Oh shit Wiz! I love you baby." They both laid back looking up at the ceiling, with smiles on their faces, about the day they had with each other, and their daughter. When Melody made it home, she kissed her husband and son. She jumped in the shower, and when she got out, she told her husband, "I think you should talk with dad a little more about life, and money. He responded, "Why? What's going on? We are doing good, and plus we have come a long way from where we once were." She replied, "Yes we are, but is it, really enough in this changing system?" Mr. Lorenzo looked at his beautiful wife, and agreed to speak with his father-in law more often. He knew his wife came from a good foundation, and certain lifestyle. Melody was doing exactly what her father did when it came to certain people and things. When it came to getting people to do what you want them to do. Which is to be cleverly and strategically persuasive without a strong indication of what's happening to the person. Melody understood greatly that her father made some powerful moves to rise from the seat of comfort and complacency which is the destroyer of greatness.

The very next morning Carlo "The Wiz" rose out of bed, and went to the restroom jumped in the shower, brushed his teeth. Next, he slipped on a pair of fresh khaki pants, and white tube socks, a fresh crisp white T-shirt, and slid his feet into his soft Italian slippers. Then, he headed to the kitchen to make himself a cup coffee. Afterwards he retrieved a cigar for the humidor, and stepped out on the front porch. Moments later his beautiful wife came out smelling fresh as a rose, and completing her daily rituals of showering, brushing her beautiful even teeth, and lotion down her sweet almond body, and joined her husband on the front porch. She kissed her husband before she took a seat next to him. Carlo "The Wiz" thought to himself *about what it took for him to become a millionaire.* He knows it wasn't easy, but it damn sure require certain important elements and actions, to receive what one truly desires. Moments later an old neighborhood friend walked up, "Morning, how is everybody felling this morning?" Those words were spoken by "High-Low." He was in his late fifties, but life has taken a toll on him, he appeared to be eighty years of age. High-Low spoke again, "Wiz, I don't mean to come at you early this morning about borrowing some money, or having a shot some of that good shit you drink. You know the liquor-store isn't open. I got to have that drink." Carlo "The Wiz" eased his into his pocket, and gave High-Low a twenty dollar bill. High-low stated, "When my boss come pick me up next week, I'll pay you back. We suppose to have a job repairing the roof on this house on the North-side." Carlo replied, "Come on High-Low, we better than that. Just do like you have been doing, and we will always be solid, dig?" He shook his head yes, and you could see the embarrassment to ask for something written on his hard life of daily struggles on his heavy wrinkled face. He was homeless, but he still had his pride. To be on top again. That's why he was known as High-Low. He was a real hustler back in his day. Driving caddies and Benzes. One day he broke the golden rule, *"don't get high on your own supply."* He spiked himself and became a heroin addict for many years. He kicked the habit years ago, due to his in and out of rehabs. He had to do 5 years on a theft charge and became a heavy drinker. After High-Low split the scene Mrs. Rodgers asked, "Why do they call him "High-Low?" Mr. Rodgers stated, "Because he always says, 'I might be down or low, but I'm not out. I will be up and high living the life, called the American Dream with green, bad bitches that's mean, and driving Benz with that OG lean on the muthafucking scene." We all have some type of vice or vices.

Whatever the mind's eye sees, is the reality that will be. Can you see yourself in those millionaire seats, or are you going to let fear keep you in a state of mental and economical poverty. If you fail to change, don't blame no one else in this life, because when you do the same, life gives you the same. Life gives you what you desire, and what you see for yourself to have. If you can picture yourself living the millionaire lifestyle daily, and remain dedicated with persistence. Then you will be one of the many, that will sit in a millionaire seat, and enjoy the life that's fulfilling and sweet.

Printed in the United States
By Bookmasters